SHAOLIN

SHAOLIN

HOW TO WIN WITHOUT FIGHTING

Using mind power to achieve peace, clarity and inner strength

BERNHARD MOESTL

Translated from the German by Anya Malhotra

AMARYLLIS

AMARYLLIS
An imprint of Manjul Publishing House Pvt. Ltd.
• C-16, Sector 3, Noida, Uttar Pradesh 201301, India
Website: www.manjulindia.com
Registered Office:
• 2nd Floor, Usha Preet Complex, 42 Malviya Nagar, Bhopal 462 003 – India
Distribution Centres
Ahmedabad, Bengaluru, Chennai, Hyderabad,
Kochi, Kolkata, Mumbai, Noida, Pune

Shaolin: How to Win Without Fighting by *Bernhard Moestl*

Originally published in German in 2008 as
Shaolin: Du musst nicht kämpfen um zu siegen by Knaur Verlag, an imprint of
Verlagsgruppe Droemer Knaur GmbH & Co. KG, Munich

English edition first published in 2022 by
Amaryllis: An imprint of Manjul Publishing House Pvt Ltd.

English translation by Anya Malhotra

This edition first published in India in 2022
Ninth impression 2025

ISBN 978-93-5543-043-4

Cover design by Misha Oberoi

Printed and bound in India by Manipal Technologies Limited

Contents

Foreword

Dear readers,

In the very heart of China, not far from the provincial capital Zhengzhou, lies the village of Shaolin. It may be small but its fame rivals that of the world's leading cities.

Ever since the Indian monk Bodhidharma established a Buddhist monastery here over 1500 years ago, myths have sprung up around this temple and its inhabitants, who are acknowledged as the invincible masters of unarmed close combat. Many even believe that the monks have superhuman powers. For almost fifteen centuries, they have been developing and perfecting the art of Shaolin kung fu.

Yet, you would be wrong if you believed that the teachings of Shaolin are essentially about fighting. Those who leave the monastery as Shaolin masters have long progressed beyond this idea. They have learnt to be aligned with their body, to respect and to use it.

They have internalised that it is their mind that energises the body—or weakens it. They have learnt that through their mind they have control over themselves and their surroundings, and that it is the mind alone that makes them invincible. Even mild anger uses up unnecessary energy that could be employed more gainfully elsewhere.

With this book, Bernhard Moestl has made it his mission to give you an insight into the Shaolin monks' way of thinking. Through thirteen life principles, he explains how you can avoid fighting and still win; and how you can cope with the hectic pace, stress and demands at a professional and personal level in a better way so your life is filled with energy and vitality.

You do not need to be a monk or live in a monastery to successfully apply these principles. You can apply them in all situations, irrespective of where you are. You must only be ready to face up to yourself, your abilities and your attitudes—and also to change these where needed.

Changing your way of thinking is not something that happens overnight. Every change needs time. Do not expect miracles from yourself, but also do not give up quickly.

Follow the Shaolin monks and find your personal path to peace, clarity and inner strength.

Gerhard Conzelmann,
President, International Shaolin Institute (regd.)

When you have the intention to renew yourself, do it every day.

Confucius

Introduction

'The art of war teaches us to rely not on the likelihood of the enemy's not coming, but on our own readiness to receive him; not on the chance of his not attacking, but rather on the fact that we have made our position unassailable.'

Sun Tzu, *The Art of War*

How this book works and how you can benefit most from it

First of all, a very warm welcome! It's wonderful that you are here! It's also wonderful that you wish to change yourself. I don't know about you, but for me 'Shaolin' has always embodied a dream. For over 1500 years, this monastery has been inextricably linked with the art of unarmed combat and with the legend of invincibility.

When I was a child, I couldn't wait to master this legendary form of martial arts. At first, simply so that I needn't fear anyone ever again. Later, it was the incredible knowledge of its practitioners that captivated me. Many sayings of the old masters have since stayed with me through my life. In my countless conversations with the monks, I finally understood that one must learn to fight so well that at some point one no longer needs to fight at all. Then it is time to face one's biggest opponent: oneself.

Change needs time

This book is divided into thirteen stand-alone chapters. Each is complete in itself and can be worked on individually. However, since there is a thematic progression in the topics, you should try and keep to the sequence as far as possible. The 'Shaolin principles' are intended not simply for reading but as a workbook. Just as one cannot learn kung fu overnight, it is also not possible to profoundly change oneself in a matter of days. The thirteen principles must become so ingrained as to become second nature, similar to fighters internalising their technique. If there is something you do not understand, don't skip it; read it once again.

For deriving maximum benefit from this book you will also need an empty notebook. Please buy an especially nice one, perhaps with an attractive cover, and write your name on it in big letters.

This notebook will be your very own personal companion, and it will know a lot about you by the end. It will contain your jottings–and they should remain just that. Within the book and at the end of every chapter, you will find several exercises and questions. Please write the answers to these in your notebook. It's best if you don't do this randomly but exactly at those places where I ask you to do so. Often we will need the answers as we proceed. It is very important to be absolutely honest while answering the questions. Write down things as they truly are. No one besides you will read the answers.

The Turkish general Mustafa Kemal Atatürk once said, 'When taking stock of a situation and evaluating measures, do not, even for a moment, avoid seeing the truth even if it is bitter.' If you work your way through this book again sometime later, you will see that your answers have changed. This book will not offer you pat solutions such as, 'If this was your answer then you must do this or that.' I, too, will not be judging your answers. You can expect to gain many insights into your own behaviour, but no rules. The change must come from within you.

'Ultimately, the biggest challenge in life,'
as Paul Gauguin said, 'is to overcome the limitations
within yourself and to go further than you
yourself could ever have imagined.'

Consider this book a journey to discover your innermost self, your friends and enemies, your potential, your limitations and much, much more. It will be my pleasure to accompany you on this journey. Let's go!

Part One

Learn to Stand

He who would learn to fly one day must first learn to stand.

Chinese proverb

Never wait until you have the time.

Chinese proverb

1. The Principle of the Present

Do not lose yourselves in the past
Do not run after the future
The past no longer is
The future has not yet come
Live in the here and now.

The Buddha

Learn to live in the here and now and become conscious of transience.

'I'll catch up with everything once I've finally retired. It's just another twelve years, I simply have to hang in there until then.' Does this sentence sound familiar to you? The idea that life at the moment isn't yet perfect but that it will become better in the foreseeable future? During the week do you live for the weekend and on weekends dread the working week ahead? And during all the other weeks of the year do you live for your holiday, or even for retirement, when you plan to finally do all those things that you believe you have missed out on?

Let's be honest: how often have you postponed doing things that you really wanted to do? Perhaps out of consideration for others, perhaps because the moment wouldn't have been suitable or because... well, why actually? And how often have you gone ahead later and done what you once found so important? 'Not often,' I hear you say. 'To be honest, hardly ever.' How often have you said to yourself, 'It's amazing that I am where I am just now; I love doing what I'm doing; it's wonderful that I have this life. What happened yesterday doesn't matter. It doesn't matter what the next day, the next hour, the next minute may bring. It's just wonderful that this very moment exists, and that I'm allowed to experience it.' Do I hear you saying again, 'Not often! To be honest, hardly ever?'

Life is all about the moment

This is the starting point of the Shaolin principle of the present. It begins here and now, at this very second and exactly at the place where you currently are.

This Shaolin principle teaches us to accept the moment. To accept everything that is linked to it, to accept what it will lead to. Accept the moment without judging it, without comparing it with the past and also with the future. Living according to Shaolin principles means to live in the moment and to regard this special moment as a wonderful, precious, transient part of life.

In one of the most important scriptures of Judaism, the *Talmud*, it is written: 'Even one lived hour is life.' That is undoubtedly true, however, the monks of the Shaolin monastery go one step further. 'Not just every lived hour, every lived moment is life,' they say. Living in the here and now means catching the moment, accepting it with gratitude and then instantly letting it go. It means understanding that not a single moment in life—whether we value it or let it pass unheeded—will ever come back.

Living in the here and now means to become aware of the moment and its transience.

It means understanding that every moment, whether it makes us happy or sad, leaves us satisfied or craving for more, cheerful or angry, must be given the respect that it deserves, for it is a part of our life.

The wise man and the tiger

Every novice in the monastery knows the story of the wise man who goes for a walk on the hillside. All of a sudden, he hears a tiger snarling some distance away but clearly approaching him. He starts running as fast as he can to escape and heads straight towards a precipice. The tiger is hot on his heels. With nowhere else to go, the man teeters along the edge of the precipice and slips. At the last moment, he is able to save himself by grabbing a root. But with the tiger above him and the abyss below, all routes of escape are blocked. At that very instant the man spies a wild strawberry directly in front of him. He plucks it, puts it in his mouth and murmurs, 'How delicious this strawberry is!'

That is what I call living in the moment! Most of us would be bewildered by the man's behaviour. Does he have nothing better to do in this situation than think of the delicious strawberry? Should he not be thinking about where his fate will lead him in the next few minutes? Well, should he really be thinking about that? What would it change about the moment? Even if the man were to be devoured by the tiger in the next minute or fall into the abyss, why should he not enjoy his life until the last moment? Why not savour the strawberry?

To accept the moment without judgement,
we must not condemn it.

No moment is good or bad, it simply is. While the man's situation does not appear promising, each moment can lead to another that has nothing to do with our expectations. Since we do not know how the story ended, we are free to tell it ourselves: the tiger loses interest in the man and wanders off. That could be one ending, could it not? Naturally, an equally possible ending is that the tiger kills the man, but it is just another alternative. Yet another alternative could be that as the man falls, he is able to latch on to a ledge, and manages to save himself.

The strawberry would not have saved the man's life, nor his interest in the strawberry. Nothing would have saved his life. The subsequent moment merely did not fulfil our expectations. And even if it had, as in the alternative ending, would that have made the moment better or worse? Neither: it was simply there. And the wise man accepted it as it was.

EXERCISE

AN EXCURSION INTO THE HERE AND NOW

Many moments will have passed as you were reading, probably without your noticing. So it's time to become conscious of the moment, to experience it, in fact to 'live' it. Are you ready? Good. Now please read through the following paragraph to the end and then put the book aside to live the moment. No, not at some point when you have the time. Here and now!

If we wish to consciously experience the moment, we must define it. We can use one second as a unit, but that would define only time, not life.

What about one breath? Take a short break and observe your breath. It may not be easy in the beginning, so use your hand to assist you by placing it on your stomach.

- Now breathe consciously. Feel how your lungs, your chest, your stomach and your abdomen fill up with oxygen.
- Hold your breath briefly, and then slowly let it escape.
- Do you feel the rise and fall of your hand? The rhythm of your life?
- Now remove your hand and focus your attention within. Is your breath still there? Do you feel the source of your life? If not, use your hand again to help you. Do you feel it?

Let us define the time between two breaths as this one moment that we want to become conscious of. Again and again. Feel your breath. Feel the moments, feel how they come and go. Can you sense your life? The here and now? Before you read on, focus on yourself for twenty moments.

You have now consciously experienced twenty moments of your life. But did you really experience the here and now? Were your thoughts with your breath and in experiencing the moment as it passed? Were they where you yourself were? Or were you also thinking of all the things that still needed to be done, what you would eat for dinner and the friend you haven't called in a long time?

Living in the moment means to focus on it fully;
to extract everything from that moment, but also to give it everything.

A student at the Shaolin monastery once approached the teacher and asked, 'Master, how do you practise living in the moment in your daily life?'

The master replied, 'When I am hungry, I eat. When I am full, I wash my bowl. When I am tired, I sleep.'

The student replied, 'Everyone does that. So does that mean that everyone practises living in the moment like you do?'

The master explained, 'No, not in the same way.'

The student asked, 'Why not in the same way?'

The master smiled, 'When others eat, they do not dare to eat. Their minds are filled with an endless number of thoughts. That is why I say, not in the same way.'

What about you? Did you experience your twenty moments like everyone else does or like the master? Did you experience them or did you squander them away because you were everywhere else except with yourself?

A good example of living beings that live by the Shaolin principles are birds. Probably all animals live by these principles but it's easiest to observe them in birds. Birds always live in the moment. They sing because spring, summer, autumn or winter is approaching. Because they are healthy and happy, because they live in the moment. When they sing, they just sing—they don't eat, feed or sleep at the same time; they do that when they eat, feed or sleep. Birds live every single moment. When one hears them sing one feels they know what makes every moment so infinitely precious: its uniqueness.

Every moment is unique

Each individual moment comes, goes and never returns. There may be similar moments, better or worse, funnier or sadder, but the one that has just passed will never come back. When we reflect on the value of the present, we must understand that what is so incredibly special is that it makes everything unique. Even if you were to read the same words again in the same book in the same way as you just did, it would no longer be identical because the time is different. No matter how we try, we can only imitate, never replicate.

So, it is not surprising that humans have always

attempted to hold onto the moment that has irretrievably passed. A study conducted about what people would save from a burning house brought out some initially surprising conclusions. Other than documents, the next most important items that people tried to salvage were their photographs. Other personal objects came later.

What is it that makes a photograph so very valuable? The fact that it can never be replaced. One can always buy various objects again or repaint a painting; but a photo, which always captures a fleeting moment, can never be recreated. Even two pictures taken half a second apart do not show the same moment. Nothing documents the transience of time as starkly as a photograph.

Western societies always seem to have been oriented towards preserving happy moments through dreams rather than increasing those moments themselves. Initially, this was done through sketches and paintings, and later through photographs. It was always the memory of this one happy moment that was sought to be preserved for posterity. But the Shaolin principle of the present teaches us that we cannot hold on to the moment. Our responsibility is to live it.

The French philosopher Jean-Paul Sartre once said, 'There may be more beautiful times, but this one is ours.'

Nonetheless, we constantly hear or read only of these 'more beautiful times'. They might well have been tougher, more difficult or required more sacrifices, but apparently, they were always better; they were different times. This is an idea that is alien to the Shaolin principle, which believes in, 'Every day is a good day'. This should not be understood from a Western perspective. A day is not good because we judge it to be so. It is also not bad because of how we perceive it. This sentence is not even an exhortation to find something good in every day.

A day, an hour, even a moment is neither good nor bad when taken as it is. It simply exists. 'Every day is a day' would perhaps be a statement we could more readily understand. In the context of the Shaolin principle that attempts to teach us not to judge the moment, 'good' is not the opposite of 'bad'.

The day, the hour, the moment is good simply because it's there. And because there is no alternative.

Life is here and now, whether we like it or not. If anything had been different at any point we would not be where we currently are. Neither you, nor I. But nothing was different, so it is entirely pointless to think about other possibilities—whether good or bad.

Even if we wake up in the morning and find ourselves ill, unemployed, alone or think we are overweight, it is what it is, and life still goes on. How you happen to feel is completely inconsequential for the time or day. The sun continues on its path, the moments of life come and go. And each time you think about why the current moment is not a good one, it is lost forever. What happens in that moment is not important, but what you personally make of it is.

Don't live your life on hold

When I tried earlier to make the time span of a moment tangible, I had first proposed a unit of one second. It is a deep-rooted human trait to want to pin everything down, to have everything neatly slotted and under control. We attempt to capture time by dividing it into seconds, hours, days and months. Everything important in our lives is allotted a specific time: Christmas, the beginning of the holidays, retirement, the delivery date of the long-awaited computer, the job interview, losing weight. And everything that does not have an allotted time becomes less important than the other things.

If we are on our way to an appointment and happen to run into someone we have been wanting to speak with for ages, then this person will still be pushed to another time slot. We will stop smoking when the New Year begins. We will familiarise ourselves with the new software when the new computer finally arrives, which should be in a few days, after all. And when we are on holiday, we will finally enjoy life again: one more week to go, seven more times to get up, five more days of going to the office. If only the week were over already! On the bright side, only two hours remain for the working day to get over, then it's another day down. One day of your life, incidentally. Do I see you nodding again? Do I hear you say that there's nothing wrong with that, after all one must be able to look forward to something? Of course one must, and one should.

But what of the time between the highlights in your life? The time between holidays? The time that you literally kill, waiting for time to pass? The time you spend on thinking that there are another hundred and seven more days of going to work before the next holidays? Have you ever considered how many moments of your life you have allowed to unthinkingly slip by because you were waiting for something? And what would happen if the holiday for which you sacrificed so much time in anticipation suddenly had to be cancelled at the last minute? So many lost moments when, in fact, each one of them could have been the most wonderful moment of your life. It is tempting to neglect the present especially when we must do something that doesn't really appeal to us or give us joy.

Living in the here and now means accepting things the way they are at that moment, and accepting from every moment what it has to offer us at that precise time.

The principle of the present teaches us to live every moment; to do things when we want to do them, when we think it necessary. Or consciously desist from doing them. It's now or never.

At some point there will no longer be a later. I remember once mentioning to a friend that we should get in touch again with a very dear colleague. It was late in the evening, and I was going to pencil in the call for the next day. 'Let's call now,' was my friend's reply, 'let's call right away.' It might sound like a convenient cliché for this story that our colleague didn't wake up one morning just a few days later, but sadly it's true. It is proof that sometimes there is no tomorrow.

People who slot their lives into various sections assume that they know the big picture: they will study until a particular point, work for a specified period, take holidays in between and then retire. Then, finally, they will be able do what they always wanted. Unrestrained freedom at last! A life worth living.

But I often wonder, how do these people know how long they are going to live? How do they know they are not wasting their entire lives waiting for something that will never happen? What makes them believe that at some point they will be compensated for all the moments they suffer now? Every day, when we wake up in the morning, we should understand clearly that whether we feel good or bad, happy or sad, whether we are alone or with someone, the secret of life lies in the present. Every moment that is not lived is lost forever. And sooner or later the day will come when it is time to go.

The present is not measured in days, not in todays and tomorrows, but in moments.

At any moment we could fall down dead and exit this game, just like that, without any reason. So, live in the here and now and never wait until you have the time.

EXERCISES

THOUGHTS ABOUT TIME

Are you able to live in the moment or do your desires and your life move in different directions? Using the questions below please reflect on how you deal with the time you have in your life.

Into which sections have you divided your life?

....

Which of them are you currently in?

....

If your life were to end in the next minute, what would you still absolutely want to do?

....

Why have you not done it so far?

....

Which was the last moment that you consciously experienced?

....

Do you wish at this moment that time would pass more quickly? If so, why?

....

If a moment were to correspond to one breath, how many moments should then have passed already?

....

The wise man is someone who, like a child, can be filled with wonder at everything.

From Tibet

2. The Principle of Mindfulness

'As a bee gathering nectar does not harm or disturb the colour and fragrance of the flower; so do the wise move through the world.'

The Buddha

Learn, that insight into others and into yourself comes through mindfulness.

In my work as a photographer I am frequently asked how to take good landscape pictures. Most people want to hear that one needs special talent, expensive equipment or at least many years of training or, better still, all of these. When they hear my reply, they are usually both astonished and taken aback.

I believe good photographers need two things: mindfulness

and humility. A good picture is one that shares your wonder with the viewer, allowing them to be a part of your moment. The viewer wants to feel your humility, bow with you, so to speak, before your subject. Which is why you must do so yourself. Then the viewer will also like your picture.

Whether you are a novice taking your first steps in photography or a professional with decades of experience under your belt: everyone is equal before the subject. You stand before the same mountains, the same meadows, the same flowers. You see the world in the same light. And yet, some photographers will take time for just a short glance through the viewfinder before pressing the shutter release to capture the memory. How much would they have been able to register in such a short glance?

Attention is a form of mindfulness

By contrast, other photographers will first simply look, and they will come back to look again and again.

They know the soft light of the morning and the evening's hues.

They know the harsh shadows at noon.

They know the landscape, the flowers, the clouds, the sky.

They know which light suits them best and which season.

When they have familiarised themselves with this landscape that will pose for them, just as portrait photographers acquaint themselves with their subjects, then it is time to look through the viewfinder and regard it more closely.

Once they have assimilated all the colours, the scent of the flowers—which will not be seen in a picture, nor the light breeze that nudges them—and valued all of this in their deepest, innermost selves, then it is time for good photographers to 'take' the picture (I find this expression very appropriate). They know that it is neither their talent, their camera nor their training that will create a good photograph: it is the landscape itself and their genuine respect for it. Once they are aware of this, the photograph will do justice to that landscape and will also appeal to viewers.

Yet, easy as it may sound, the principle of mindfulness is a difficult principle. It is an idea that one must slowly learn and can only gradually grasp.

As the saying goes in China, if you want to draw bamboo then you must draw bamboo all your life. Perhaps then you will be able to draw bamboo.

Of course, you could go to every tree and to every bush and flower and say, 'I am mindful of you.' You could go up to every person, to every stone and stream and say, 'I am mindful of you.' People who know you would admire you as someone who has understood this difficult principle and seems to be living it.

But you yourself would probably find it a bit weird rather

than deriving any joy from it because your thinking would not have changed. It would simply be an empty gesture that has nothing to do with true mindfulness. One cannot just wake up one fine day and turn into a great landscape photographer, and in the same way one cannot experience mindfulness in a day.

EXERCISES

HOW TO LEARN MINDFULNESS

The path to mindfulness begins at the point when you start becoming aware of yourself, to 'feel' yourself; when you become conscious of your body and its capabilities. Let's try this out. Not later or some other time... You know the drill.

- Start with your hands. It doesn't matter if you are sitting, standing or lying down at this moment. It is very likely that you are holding this book. Perhaps you have it lying in front of you and have propped your head in one or both hands. Do you always read the way you are reading now?
- Now start by focusing on your hands, sensing them. Consciously feel them all the way to your fingertips. Do you notice a change? Do you feel the book that these fingers are holding? Do you sense that you are

becoming aware of yourself? Then let's proceed.

- Allow the feeling to travel slowly over your arms up to your chest. Back to the fingers again and then again to the chest. Slowly.
- Do you feel your breath? Pay attention to it. Breathe with the ribs, expand your chest, allow it to fill with air. Breathe also with your stomach and consciously press down your diaphragm. Do you feel how your chest and stomach expand and air fills your body? Pause briefly and then exhale.
- Did you notice that your conscious focus on your breath made your lower body heavier and more stable? If you are sitting, follow the feeling from your pelvis down to your glutes.
- Straighten your upper body and shift your centre of gravity down to your buttocks. Do you feel the contact with the seat?
- Now bring your feet to the ground. Let the feeling slowly wander along your legs to the feet and the soles. If you are not able to manage in the first attempt, simply try again. The principle of mindfulness is difficult only because we have unlearned it for so long. Back to your feet: the soles of both feet should be on the floor. Leave them loose, do not press them down. Simply feel their connection with the ground.

- If you now simultaneously focus on your feet and buttocks you will realise that you are sitting very, very firmly. Nothing can shake you in this position. And you will notice that mindfulness creates a surprising and deep sense of peace.
- Now bring your attention back, over your legs, pelvis, your breath and arms to your hands; and feel the book again.

It has been 1500 years since the Shaolin monastery and its mastery over hand-to-hand combat were established under the Indian monk Bodhidharma—1500 years, in which the monks at the monastery have elevated the principle of mindfulness to one of their rules of life, making them the most revered warriors of all time. Novices at the monastery must learn not only to look after and maintain their bodies, but also to recognise and employ the body's thousand abilities. On a slippery surface they must be able to feel their grounding, to consciously control every joint of their fingers and toes. They must be able to control their gaze and the tempo of their breathing. And they must learn to execute every movement deliberately and with purpose.

Good fighters leave nothing to chance. They will always observe the most important rule, namely that there is no rule, there is just the principle of mindfulness.

Let me give you an example. If you want to become

a landscape photographer, you would perhaps ask me for some tips. I could tell you not to position the horizon in the middle of the frame but to place it in the lower third. It makes for a stronger composition. You would follow my rule and not position the horizon in the middle but in the lower third. Would that have anything to do with mindfulness? Would you take better pictures because of it? Probably not. But if I were simply to tell you to pay attention to the position of the horizon in every picture, that would be entirely different. Pay attention to the effect, experiment with having the horizon above, below and in the middle. Ultimately it is your photograph; what can my rules achieve? If you prefer the horizon in the middle then that is exactly where it belongs. But not if you have merely forgotten to think about it. Whether you observe or ignore rules, do so consciously.

Being mindful of oneself means to pick from amongst the vast array of available options and to choose that precise one, which is most suitable in a given situation.

It also means knowing as many of these options as possible. Now that you have experienced mindfulness towards yourself, it is time to proceed further. After all, you are not the only person in the world. So follow me into a glorious, sunny afternoon on an equally glorious and sunny spring day.

Mindfulness towards creation

Do you see the meadow with thousands of bright flowers in bloom all around us? How they glisten and gleam? The sheer abundance of flowers? I have seen them too. It made me happy: the spring, the lovely warm weather and the flowers. Usually that would have been the end of the matter for me as far as the meadow and the beauty of the flowers were concerned.

But this time a person, whose deep knowledge of the essence of things has often surprised me, said, 'Of course the flowers are beautiful. Don't forget how hard they work at it. They have to shine and smell sweet so that they are visited by the bees.' That insight was simply amazing. Every single one of the millions of flowers is trying! Every single one attempts to glisten and outdo the others in fragrance so that it is not forgotten by the bees. Every one of those flowers is a living being like me. And every one of those flowers is also making an effort for me. It wants to be liked by the bees and it wants to be liked by me. It is happy when I see it, notice it and when it gives me joy.

That was the moment I learnt mindfulness. You could say, of course, that all this is nonsense. Flowers are fragrant because over the course of time they have simply evolved that way. It is the old principle of the survival of species. And you would undoubtedly be right. Without the bees the flowers simply could not survive.

Mindfulness creates happiness

But does it also explain why we can be happy about it? We could be quite indifferent to everything and our indifference would change nothing. The sun would continue to rise and set in a blaze of colour, flowers would bloom and smell as sweet, birds would chirp and life would go on as always. Everything would happen as evolution intended. Yet we have the choice to observe, to marvel and be happy. If this opportunity for happiness exists and it can make our lives so much more gratifying, why should we not use it? In any case, in our lifetime we are no longer going to find out what the reason is.

A person who embodied how one can derive all one's vitality from this principle was Francis of Assisi. Of advanced age, seriously ill and marked with the wounds of Jesus Christ on his hands and feet, making it impossible for him to grasp or walk, he composed one of the most beautiful hymns to mindfulness. We tend now to condescendingly dismiss it as the 'canticle of the sun', but Francis called his text the 'canticle of the creatures'. Nothing escapes his consideration: not the sun, moon or stars, without whose light we could not see; nor the animals and bright flowers, nor even people and the Creator of them all. At the height of his incurable physical suffering, Francis of Assisi was also able to find great joy through mindfulness.

The Shaolin principle of mindfulness teaches us to understand that nothing, absolutely nothing, is self-evident, even if it appears to be so and we accept it as such.

This kind of joy, in fact, came very naturally even to you when you were young. Children can stand amidst nature for hours and observe a waterfall, the wisps of a dandelion or an anthill, silent and filled with wonder at their new discovery. A discovery that will be just as new and fascinating at the next visit. This is a path to inner peace that we lost somewhere along the way to becoming adults but which is certainly worthwhile to rediscover. The Shaolin principle teaches us to regard everything in this world as something special. As the monks of Shaolin say, it teaches us that mindfulness leads to deeper insights and to awakening.

Once, so the story recounted in the monastery goes, a young monk wanted to know from his master what mindfulness really meant.

'Mindfulness,' the master replied, 'means mindfulness.'

Being non-judgemental

Mindfulness encompasses attention and respect: attention to the moment and respect for everything around us. But, as we have already seen in the principle of the present, there is one thing it does not mean, namely to judge. Passing judgement clouds our minds and instantly blunts the edge of this powerful sword. We should have respect not for *how* things are but *that* they are.

Neither should we differentiate in the quantum of respect that we show to different people. Rather, we must respect without discriminating between those who supposedly are subordinate to us and those we believe we must look up to. We must respect our friends in the same measure as we respect our opponents, and we must respect ourselves to the same degree as everyone else.

In China, there is mindfulness in the rituals of daily life. If we observe two people meeting for the first time, the first thing they do is exchange visiting cards. They give and take the visiting cards with both hands, standing and bowing slightly. Without (yet) knowing whom they are facing, they show each other mutual respect.

The young novices at Shaolin must continuously prove their skills to their masters. Before they begin such an exercise, the candidates bow deeply in the direction of the examiners. It may surprise you—although it shouldn't any longer—that these monks, who are much older and experienced, return the salutation by bowing equally deeply.

Have you just caught yourself thinking that it really is a big deal if a quasi-superior bows to someone who is below them in rank? Do you think it is the younger novices who should be showing respect to their teachers, who are superior to them, rather than the other way around? You must then understand that even the principle of being non-judgemental is a difficult one—partly because it is so deeply ingrained in us.

Trusting our perceptions

Since childhood we have learnt to classify, divide, categorise and judge. We learn which plants are useful and which are weeds, which ones we allow to grow and the ones that must be pulled out. We learn about good animals and bad ones, of friends and foes, of good and evil, of black and white. We learn what is possible and what cannot be, what one should do and what to avoid. We learn that there are small, weak opponents and big, strong ones.

Amidst this profusion of judgements, we unlearn heeding our own observations, our own assessment, especially when it contradicts prevailing wisdom. You are likely to consider a big, burly man as a strong opponent and a delicate child to be weak.

> Please take your notebook and write down five characteristics of a strong opponent and five characteristics of a weak one. Don't hesitate, don't overthink, just write. It is your notebook after all. But do review your opinion from time to time.

How surprised many people would be to learn that a small ten-year-old novice in Shaolin can overpower five grown men!

The principle of mindfulness teaches us that even things that don't seem possible can happen. It teaches us that we must be objective and unbiased towards every moment and every living being, even if we will often find this difficult. And that we must never underestimate our opponents, but also never overestimate them. If we carelessly judge an opponent to be stronger than they are, that might actually make them more powerful.

Gauging others accurately

Let us assume that someone wrongly claims you owe them money. You obviously don't pay them, and one fine day you receive a letter with a notice for immediate payment and the threat of legal proceedings should you fail to comply. The harsh and pompously worded letter is signed by a Dr John Q. Public. Now, my question is, what subject did Dr Public study? 'Law, of course,' I hear you say. 'What else?' You apparently owe money, he writes this letter and threatens with legal proceedings. But what if you simply overestimated him and he has a doctorate in biology, art history or languages? Just because you ostensibly owe money and he has the title 'Dr' doesn't mean he has to be a lawyer, right?

Had you not judged but acted following the principle of mindfulness, you would have drawn no conclusions initially. Subsequently, you would have found out that Dr Public merely had an honorary doctorate from a university in Russia and was actually a retired technician. You would then have reacted appropriately and formulated a suitable response. But in the former case, you might have ended up paying the money to avoid any further problems. So do not underestimate your opponents but also do not overestimate them. Face them with mindfulness.

Respecting your opponents means being able to size them up. Being non-judgemental means being able to assess them. Facing them with mindfulness means being able to defeat them.

The principle of mindfulness teaches us to recognise our own abilities and potential as well as those of our opponent. It teaches us that being respectful allows us to be filled with wonder, and wonder leads to joy. It teaches us that being mindfully connected with everything around us can make you invincible.

EXERCISES

USING ALL THE SENSES

The following questions are intended to help you learn mindfulness. Try to answer them all even if some might appear difficult at first.

What do the flowers of cherry, apricot and apple trees smell like?

....

Take a glass of water. What does it smell like? How does it taste?

....

Can you distinguish between individual roses in a bunch by their smell?

....

Please answer this question spontaneously: Who do you feel should be given a lot of respect?

....

Why?

....

And who, in your opinion, deserves very little respect?

....

Why?

....

Next time you are with several people, try and guess their profession based on their clothes, posture, behaviour and language. Ask them about it later. How many did you guess correctly?

....

Stand still wherever you are at this very moment. What do you see?

....

What do you consider weeds?

....

....

If you are resolute, consider it done.

Confucius

3. The Principle of Resoluteness

Necessity takes precedence over all laws.

From China

Learn to do things wholeheartedly or to let them be.

'When you draw your sword, in your mind you must be prepared to kill the opponent. Even when you parry the opponent's blow, your grip must remain unchanged and your hand must not cramp. At all times you must grip the sword with the intent to kill your opponent.'

Miyamoto Musashi, who wrote these words, is considered among the greatest swordsmen of all time. The samurai was believed to be invincible after he killed more than sixty challengers. He devoted the rest of his life in seventeenth-century Japan to the study of swordsmanship.

Obviously, it is not the intention of this book to encourage you to draw a sword, or worse, to kill someone. That would neither be acceptable nor in keeping with the times, and it would only land you in trouble. The sword in today's times is invisible, concealed in our heads. It is the principle of resoluteness.

EXERCISES

TAKING DECISIONS

Before we proceed, please take out your notebook.

- Start a new page and write down a few things that you are really determined to do. These should not be things like purchasing a new car or a more powerful computer, but personal resolutions, such as 'quit smoking,' 'change my hair style,' or 'find a new job'. Write down ten such things. Done?
- Good. Now go over your list again and strike out everything that you aren't absolutely determined to do. I mean entries where you think, 'Yes, I really should some time...'
- Finally strike out everything that you can't yet do, i.e., entries such as, 'After I get married I will...,' which are linked to a specific occurrence.
- After a thorough vetting, you should be left with three lines. Again write down these three things, which you

feel you are really determined to do, below the other entries.

What you now have in your notebook are three lines that express what you would like to do or what you think is necessary to do. But there is nothing here about what you are truly determined to do, because then you would have done it already.

Hear me out before you protest. I want to show you that there is a vast difference between 'wanting' something and 'being determined' to do something. First of all, of course, wanting is the most important step to becoming determined. Second, I am sure your notebook does not contain entries like 'water the plants', 'go to work tomorrow' or 'turn off the radio before going to bed'. Why not? Because that is something you are really determined to do. Your resolve is so strong that you take it for granted.

Naturally, there will have been times when you got up in the morning and considered not going to work. You decided that you would call in sick some day soon, finally be able to sleep in and take two or three days off to do what you really wanted. With all the recent overtime hours that you hadn't claimed, you needn't even have a bad conscience about it. But despite everything, it remained just a wish. What you were really determined to do was to go to work, and that is exactly what you did.

That is the difference between 'wanting' and 'being determined'.

- Now, with this in mind, write down five things in your notebook that you are truly determined to do. You will undoubtedly find more but cut them down to five lines. You might be a little surprised that they appear to be ordinary, everyday things. Perhaps you've noted the ten minutes of your lunch break that belong only to you, which you allow no one to invade: ten minutes during which you even switch off your mobile phone so that you really have time for yourself. Did you write down, 'Tidy up my desk before leaving office?' Do the daily cooking and cleaning? Take out the garbage? All the things that you are so determined about that you do them as a matter of course, although there is nothing really matter of course about them. What will be left on your list are only those things that you are truly determined to do.
- Now re-read the ten lines in your notebook and evaluate them by asking the following question: how difficult is it to dissuade me from doing this? For example, if it is very difficult to dissuade you from ironing the laundry then put two crosses against that line. If it is somewhat difficult then put one cross, and if your reaction is 'are you nuts?' then put none. Please be

honest. Your evaluation should reflect reality rather than what you would like it to be.

- If you now look at the results you will probably notice that there are more crosses in the upper lines compared to the ones further down. As you can see, you rate your wishes and what you consider necessities differently.
- Now write down the line with the most crosses and note underneath it why it is so difficult to dissuade you from it. Do the same with the second and third.
- Now move on to the things that you are not very determined about. Please write below them why it would be easy to dissuade you from doing them.
- And lastly, please write a few words about what distinguishes your intentions. What I mean is, e.g., 'I go to work because that is my duty, but I do not ask for a raise because it is still too premature for that.'

You will have realised by now that there are some things that simply have to be done and some that you would like to do. The difference between your perception and assessment also influences your actions.

Interestingly, the things that we find easier are not the ones that are more difficult to dissuade us from doing. On the contrary, we are often more determined about the difficult things and allow ourselves to be diverted from the easier ones.

Let's take your work again as an example to illustrate this. You plan to take a day off so as to have a long weekend. You've even worked extra hours for this in advance. Two days before your short break you are told that the company needs you urgently and to please shift the date of your leave. This is the moment of truth, for this will tell you whether you simply wanted to take the day off or whether you were really determined to do so.

Wanting without determination is like a heavy millstone that you hang around your own neck. It takes up an enormous amount of energy that you will lack elsewhere.

Objectively, it would probably be easier for you not to go to work and to stay at home or wherever and enjoy the day. You wouldn't be sacrificing anything by not going to work.

But in fact, in this situation it will be very much more difficult to dissuade you from going to work (although that is precisely what you do not want to do) rather than to take the holiday that you had worked and arranged for so far in advance. In other words, you merely had the desire to take this day off but not the resolve. Or has it ever happened to you that something came up while you were on your way to work and, on an impulse, you then actually went elsewhere?

I am going to use an example to illustrate this. Let's assume you want to switch to a healthier diet. You intend to do this but are not really determined. As a consequence, your diet will not change but you will spend five times as much time shopping for food. You will deliberate thrice about every 'unhealthy' item before you finally place it in your shopping basket. Thoughts like, 'I shouldn't really, but…' along with convincing counter-arguments will fill your head, as will a guilty conscience, self-reproach and envious glances at those who seem to have made it. And of course, finally the firm resolve to do everything differently starting tomorrow.

What do you get out of this? Your diet did not change and nor did anything else. But you cluttered your head and had much less focus left for what is of substance.

Wanting alone does not get you what you want

Sometimes, wanting without determination can even land you in serious danger. Tourists travelling to remote or unsafe parts of the world might think they should take a gun along. The idea being that if they are attacked and there is a threat to their lives, they would at least have a chance of defending themselves against the attacker.

Unfortunately, it's not quite as straightforward as that. What is necessary to actually defend oneself—apart from perfect mastery of the weapon—is the absolute determination to kill the opponent if needed. This means drawing the weapon with the willingness to shoot immediately. While it will never be our goal to take a life, the death of the attacker in this case is a collateral risk.

If we simply wave the pistol about threateningly, the sight of a weapon would likely make the attacker even more aggressive. The empty threat coupled with the attacker's determination could well have fatal consequences for the tourist. They would die because they wanted to defend themselves but did not have the determination to actually use the weapon. It would have been better to leave the pistol out of the equation in this case.

The third Shaolin principle teaches us to either do things wholeheartedly or not at all. It teaches us that we should do only what we are truly determined—and willing—to do.

In the Shaolin monastery too, the monks constantly train and test this ability. The power with which the bare hand of a kung fu fighter slices through several bricks apparently effortlessly is the power of determination at work. If, with the same physical force, the fighter was to hesitate even for a fraction of a second, a broken hand would be the best outcome. The fighter must not just want to break the bricks, he must be fully determined to do so.

We have seen that resolve is an immensely powerful device, both in confrontations with others and equally in our struggles with ourselves. I will now show you how to strengthen it. We will begin with a situation in which our two biggest inner rivals—wanting and not-wanting—are in conflict. We will exclude 'I do want to but…' and other variations of this here because they belong to the category of not-wanting.

Laying the path to the goal

When we prepare for a confrontation, we outline our goal and, more importantly, the path to reach that goal. Knowing the path and following it can make the difference between success and failure and, in extreme cases, between life and death.

I once learned during a survival training course that when one is in an emotionally fraught and extremely difficult situation, such as being caught in an avalanche, one must try to clear one's head for a short while. During those lucid moments one makes a plan for the further course of action and commits it to memory. This is the plan for survival. It doesn't matter how absurd or senseless this plan might appear later when things are confusing; one must stick to it at all costs. It is important to cling to the plan and continue along the path one originally decided on.

Musashi said, 'One may study a path with zeal, yet if one deviates from it, however slightly, it is no longer the true way, even if one considers it a good way. Those who do not strictly remain on the true path and allow themselves even a small diversion will reach a dead end. This should be reflected on.'

Let us return to our example of healthy eating. Your goal is to have a good and balanced diet. The path to achieve it requires stopping buying things that you yourself regard as unhealthy. This, then, is the plan you make. So, when you are shopping, even if you have a sudden craving and hundreds of arguments in favour pop into your mind, you will no longer buy those items.

This is the position you must always return to if suddenly your entire plan seems ridiculous and absurd. Remember that you decided on it in a moment unswayed by emotion and therefore you simply no longer buy anything unhealthy. If on occasion you are tempted and think, 'Just this once it won't really matter…,' then you must imagine banging your hand down on a table and saying loudly and clearly: 'Out!' Do this until the inner demons give peace. It may sound funny, but it works!

Staying on course

Apart from having a plan, it is important to be consciously consistent. This means that if you decide to do something every day, you must actually do it every day even if at times you don't feel like doing so. For example, if you find an excuse even one single time not to do your daily five minutes of morning exercises, from then onwards you will find some reason every day not to exercise.

Nip excuses in the bud with a firm 'Out!' This way your plan will become a habit over time and ultimately an integral part of you. It doesn't matter whether you plan to change your diet, stop smoking or want to learn ten new foreign words every day for your vacation abroad. The path to achieve your goal is always the same. By banging your fist on the imaginary table, the sword of your resolve is ready to use.

Weak resolve spells opportunity for an opponent

As I mentioned earlier, wanting something without being determined is like having a millstone around your neck. It immobilises you and in the hands of an opponent it could even become a dangerous weapon to ultimately defeat you.

Company X launches a new product that you have absolutely no need for. What will company X, which now becomes your opponent, do? It will find out that you have no interest in buying the product but also that you aren't determined *not* to buy it. It will then constantly try to show you the attractiveness and advantages of the product and push you into a tussle with yourself.

The diabolical thing is that company X now no longer needs to expend any further efforts on you because you are already doing their job for them. 'I really don't need it,' you start thinking, 'but if I did have it, I could do this and that, although I won't really do those things, but…' And finally, you buy the product that you have no use for so that you have peace from the tussle in your mind.

In the 'Water Scroll' section from *The Book of Five Rings*, Miyamoto Musashi writes: 'It is important […] to know the enemy's sword and not to be distracted by insignificant movements of his sword. You must study this.' The opponent's sword is his determination to sell you the product. Had you been equally determined from the very beginning not to buy the product, it would never have become an issue and you need not have wasted either mind space or money. It is very important never to underestimate an opponent who has time.

'Determination has nothing to do with the length of the years,' say the monks of Shaolin.

What they mean is that a true decision is one that remains unchanged even after sleeping on it many times. A furious, 'I'm never going to touch this or that again…' does not last longer than the anger.

The martial arts technique of kung fu has reached an unmatched level of perfection over the centuries. Then why, in a fight where both combatants are equally skilled, does one manage to win? Because the opponent's concentration wavers for a brief moment and they make a mistake that will decide the outcome of the combat.

Lethargy weakens resolve

Another way to subvert the resoluteness of an opponent is to exploit their lethargy. You might have heard that a frog thrown into a pot of boiling water will immediately jump out. But placed in cold water that is slowly heated, the same frog can be cooked to death.

So, what does this have to do with you? Company Y wants to double its service charges. If it does this overnight, even the most weak-willed person will immediately decide to find another provider. The same price increase spread over a period of time diminishes this resolve. 'It's only ten per cent more, and everything is getting more expensive,' you convince yourself ten times. Until the company has achieved its objective.

> Please write down five things in your notebook where you are a frog. Also note why you allow yourself to be boiled to death and where you need to change something.

Up until this point we have become acquainted with the principle of resoluteness as a defence technique and successfully tested it. But it can do much more because it is also a principle of action. If you are caught committing a legal offence, it is highly probable that the officer will want you to pay a fine.

Irrespective of whether it is a large or small amount, you will probably refuse to pay up and will be sent a notice. All along, you are aware that there is no way to avoid paying the fine, so you have created a completely unnecessary problem for yourself. The notice will arrive, it will lie around for a few days and then you will pay with interest. Apart from causing you a few days of annoyance plus having to go to the bank, you gained nothing.

The Shaolin principle teaches us to accept things that we cannot change for the moment and to do what is necessary. My grandmother, to whom I owe so much, is the one who taught me the principle of action. She never reacted to any of the silly things I did when I was young by saying, 'How could you do that?' or 'Now, let me see how you fix that!' She would always ask, 'What do we need to do now?' And then she would proceed to do exactly that. Everything else would be dealt with later. I'm sure other people would have itched to lecture me many times, but she never gave them a chance.

Act, don't react

The principle of action also teaches us that there are very few people who act and many who react. Those who act are in a better position to begin with. They determine the rules of the game, select the place where it will play out and prepare themselves mentally for confrontation. Since they are the ones who choose the time and place, they arrive well-rested, survey the area and then strike when they think it is opportune. The defenders can only try to defend.

Naturally, the attackers will do everything to preserve this advantage. They will hide their true intentions by manipulating the defenders. People tend to look up to doers and forget that every single one is also just a person with weaknesses, fears, problems and bad dreams. 'He knows what he's doing,' people think, or 'I'll wait for what she has to say.' If someone decides to act as an expert on life in distant galaxies, they will gain recognition and will soon be consulted on other topics as well. Not because of their knowledge, since that cannot be verified, but because they acted and by doing so made themselves an expert. You might subsequently also act by putting forward relevant arguments to counter their theories, but you will remain in second place because you only reacted.

The Shaolin principle of resoluteness teaches us that those who act change the course of the world and the lives of other people.

As long as you merely react, such people will continue to tell you what you should and should not do. The great philosopher Lao Tzu once said that a journey of a thousand miles begins with a single step. The principle of resoluteness reminds us to take precisely this first step.

EXERCISES

TEST YOUR RESOLVE

Determination can be learnt. The questions below will show you where you currently stand. Come back to these often to observe the changes in you.

What things do you do only if someone else asks you to do them?

....

Why is that so (in each case)?

....

Of the things that you would ideally like to do every day, which things do you allow yourself to be talked out of?

....

If you want to do them, why do you allow yourself to be side-tracked?

....

When was the last time your opponents chose the time and place of an encounter?

....

How did they manage to do this?

....

Why did you not recognise this tactic?

....

When was the last time you chose the time and place of an encounter?

....

How did you manage?

....

When was the last time you came second because someone else was more determined?

....

When was the last time you prevailed in a situation because you were more determined?

....

Close your eyes. What you see belongs to you.

Günter Eich

4. The Principle of Detachment

The origin of all suffering is greed and desire.

The Buddha

Learn, that greed makes you predictable, vulnerable and susceptible to coercion.

Detachment has a much wider meaning in Asia than in the West. Europeans often understand it as consciously foregoing something. The Asian way of life regards detachment as a path to freeing oneself from the idea that it is actually possible to own something. When you have reached a stage where you genuinely do not wish to possess anything, you will no longer suffer.

Imagine that one day the bell rings and an important-looking person is at your door. The person shows you an ID card stating that they are empowered to take away everything you own without assigning any reasons: your TV, car, golf set, designer suit, the expensive watch, everything. Without waiting, they begin to pack up your things. A terrible thought, isn't it? Imagine yourself in that situation. What would you be thinking? What would you try to save at all costs or to hide? How would you react?

Please take your notebook and write down five feelings that you associate with this situation. These could be indifference or anger or helplessness. Be honest with yourself and identify those five uppermost feelings that you associate with it. Now, are there any of these feelings you wish you had more often? If so, please note the number below. Next to it write the number of unpleasant feelings. I suspect that the number of negative feelings will outweigh any positive ones.

How many negative feelings arise from the fear of not having or getting enough? How much suffering is caused by the desire to possess things that one simply cannot have? Let me be provocative: just look into your notebook. 'The origin of all suffering,' the Buddha said, 'is greed.'

Greed makes you helpless

You might ask why it is not possible to own something. Here is a brief example. A while ago there was a storm during which heavy rain and winds devastated parts of an uninhabited section of a forest. Trees were uprooted and struck by lightning, nature wreaked havoc in the truest sense of the word. The next day, the newspapers reported, 'Thousands of trees uprooted. Storm causes damage worth millions in forest.' I found it strange. Who faced the damage? Not the forest surely? It seemed unlikely to me that the trees actually belonged to anyone. I would be more inclined to believe that someone had thought they would simply acquire those trees. That person failed to realise that there are things in this world that cannot be owned. What they were left with ultimately was the damage and all the negative feelings of loss.

Greed, fundamentally, is a deeply human emotion. In fact, it is so human that it distinguishes us from all other creatures on earth. Have you ever heard of a lion who killed ten zebras more than he could eat so that he might sell them later? Of course you haven't. A lion, like all other animals, lives in the moment and knows that there will always be enough available for it to comfortably survive. The greed to have more and more is something reserved for us humans.

The fourth Shaolin principle teaches us that it is precisely this greed that makes us vulnerable, predictable and susceptible to coercion. Those who do not have their greed in check give others power over themselves and their emotions and are thus easier to attack.

The monk and the general

In the Shaolin monastery, a story is told of a general who was travelling on horseback with his soldiers. One day he chanced upon a Zen monk who had just entered into a state of deep meditation.

The general was outraged and shouted, 'Hey! You there! Monk! Get out of my way!'

The monk continued to sit motionless and silent.

'Are you deaf? Didn't you hear? I said, get out of my way!'

But the monk continued to sit motionless and still.

Looking down from his horse the general threatened him, 'Perhaps you don't know who is before you? Here is a person who can kill you any moment without batting an eyelid.'

That is when the monk looked up and said, 'Perhaps you do not know whom you have before you. Before you sits a person who can die at any time without batting an eyelid!'

Detachment frees you

What does this story have to do with detachment? A lot. On one side is the seemingly all-powerful general, filled with greed for power and recognition. He is like the person at the beginning of the chapter and believes he has the power to impose his will on others by threatening to take everything away from them, even their life. Opposing him is a meditating monk. There is nothing in the world that the general can really take away from the monk. The monk's detachment is so extreme that he does not cling even to his own life. He is prepared to give it up in the blink of an eye. How powerful is the general now?

There is a wise saying that greed makes people predictable. Our greed gives others an opportunity to exercise power over us. Had the general not encountered the austere monk but someone like you or me, how would the episode have played out? Probably the general would have had his way.

Expectation allows you to be manipulated

Desire, just like detachment, is not always about material things. It can be something as simple as me not reciprocating your greeting one fine day and ignoring you. You would be irritated by my behaviour because you expected a reaction. I would now know exactly what to do if I wanted to provoke you into making a mistake later because of your anger. Similarly, desire makes you vulnerable to coercion: if you do not do as I wish, I will take away something that belongs to you, like your money, your car, your job.

Of course, everyone needs to make a living, but how far are you willing to go? Once, a crane operator was at work when a storm hit the city in which I live. The storm escalated into a hurricane but the man continued to work. His boss had forbidden him to leave because the site had to be completed. Unsurprisingly, the storm was stronger than the crane and it toppled, killing the crane operator on the spot. I have often asked myself why he placed his work above the danger of losing his life. Those who are in a position to give something to others possess power. There is no difference in this respect between humans and animals.

'To tame a wild animal,' an old, Native American once told me, 'You must confine it in a pit and starve it. When it is practically dying you go and feed it. You must make sure that it sees you bringing it food. That animal will not leave your side for the rest of its life.' Someone who is in a position to deprive others of something has even more power. I am not referring to robbers or thieves who take things from others to make money. In fact, people who take something solely to exercise power have no interest in the object itself—they will have hardly any use for it. Their interest lies in exploiting the opponent's greed to achieve their objective.

Even the strongest opponent cannot gain any power over someone whom they can deprive of nothing.

The famous Japanese warriors, the samurai, did not consider death as something to be feared. Death was considered one with life, not a contradiction. Transcending life and death was considered part and parcel of every fight. Losing one's life in combat was the greatest honour. As in the case of the meditating monk, there was nothing anyone could take away from these elite soldiers. The fighting prowess of the samurai is legendary, even today.

EXERCISES

WHAT IS INDISPENSABLE?

- Please write in your notebook what you would not want to forego in your life under any circumstances. Write down about ten points and leave space of half a page after each.
- Now, under each point write No. 1 and note alongside why exactly you find it indispensable. Why do you need it? You must be absolutely honest: if you need the new car to impress your colleagues at work then write that down.
- Under No. 2 note down what you had to give in return to own it. Don't note down any amount but

things like hours of work, the old car, or how much time of your life.

- Now under No. 3 please write down what exactly would change in your life if you did not have it. What disadvantage would you be put to if it were taken away from you? To stay with the example of the car to impress your colleagues with, what would change if you could no longer impress them?
- Is the advantage you gain by owning it worth the fear that the car could get scratches, become damaged in an accident or get stolen? Note down your answer to this question under No. 4.
- Now order your list in sequence. Number what is most important with 1 and so on. Please read on only when you have completed this.

You will notice that I completely avoided using the words 'things' or 'objects' when describing this exercise. Is there anything on your list that no one can take away from you? Feelings such as joy or love? Good conversations? Real friends and people you are close to?

I still vividly remember a situation in which a thief stole all my belongings. I was travelling in a foreign country and, in the blink of an eye, I was left with nothing but my flight ticket and passport. No money, no sleeping bag, no clothes, nothing at all. Having nothing was quite a strange feeling at first. All of a sudden, you feel naked and lost. People walk past, they have a home, clean clothes and money to buy anything. You feel that everyone can see you are penniless.

Once I had reconciled to the idea that I could not change my situation, I experienced the most carefree weeks of my life. I could sleep wherever I wanted without having to tie my luggage to my legs like everyone else did for fear of it being stolen. The people to whom I recounted my story helped in whichever way they could. Those who could give no money offered food or clean clothes or even simply good wishes. I was free in a way I had never been before. It was then that I understood how little one really needs in life.

Declutter your life

It is possible to declutter your life without having to give up everything all at once. One can only progress from external to internal order, as the educational reformer Maria Montessori said in so many words.

How many things that you've wanted to get rid of for a long time are still lying around in your home? Things that you don't throw away only because they were presents, souvenirs or whatever? If your bad conscience is the only reason that these things are still around then get rid of them. Do it now. Those who gave you these things don't clutter up their homes either. If you are one of those people who turns everything over thrice and then puts it back because it might just come in handy some time, you need to start taking drastic action. All the things that you haven't missed until now are things you won't be needing in the future either, and they can go.

The deep-rooted need to own is a constant battle in which there are few winners and many losers. The victors in this battle ultimately are those who can better conceal their greed.

If you target your opponent's greed you hit them at their most vulnerable spot.

An employer might want to increase profits by getting a very skilled employee to do unpaid overtime since many customers come only because of this specific employee. The employer therefore threatens to fire the employee if they don't comply. Fearing for their job, the employee agrees to the demands made by the boss—and has thereby already lost the battle. Aware now of the employee's weakness, the boss will continue making demands to extract even more money, always with the unspoken threat of dismissal. At some point, however, the pressure on the employee will be so great as to make them quit. The net result: both would have lost. Had the employee taken a step back initially and assessed the situation unclouded by their own need, the battle would have ended differently. They would have recognised the employer's greed and become aware of their own worth. Why threaten to dismiss a person one needs so desperately? But it may also not be a good idea for the employee to yield to their own greed and demand a pay raise in this situation without offering something in return. It would be better for them to find a mutually acceptable solution along with a bonus from the employer.

There are people who will persuade you to buy the more expensive device that you really like but don't need at all by saying it is definitely superior. They are playing on your greed and disguising their own. You will know you are the loser when you realise that the purchase was unnecessary. Please write down five things in your notebook where you lost in this way.

Have you heard of the famous question about what you would wish for if you had just one wish? I am now asking you exactly that. Reflect briefly and write down your wish in your notebook.

Many people, and perhaps you are one of them, wish for wealth. Enough to buy whatever they want at any time without having to think about their account balance. 'XY has so much more money than I do. All I want is as much as they have.' Let's turn this around. You are relatively well-to-do because you have more money in a month than many other people have in a year. For these people you are the rich XY to whom they look up. Does that make you feel happier? I have met people on my travels who possessed only the bare minimum to survive, and yet they had so much happiness and joy that they were able to share some with me. The principle of the present has taught you to live in the here and now. Let me put the question differently. What is giving you joy at precisely this moment? What is making you happy just now? You may realise to your surprise that it is not a material thing.

In your notebook write the heading, 'What I own that money can't buy.' Once again, find at least ten points and note them down. Do you now know how rich you actually are?

Addiction to attention

Excessive desire for attention and affection can also be a dangerous weapon in the hands of an opponent. So many people these days start having doubts about the legitimacy of their existence if no one contacts them at least once every five minutes. Many can't survive without receiving constant validation at work. They slog away until they burn out, but there is still more overtime, more stress, more work! 'Have to go in to work early all of next week, there is so much to do!' Needless to say, all this is without any extra pay, after all, 'My boss needs me!' The boss will naturally be rubbing their hands in glee at having such employees.

Such people are manipulated by those whom they look up to, who pretend to give them the attention they seek. They do not realise that they are being used and that in the long run they are losing more than they gain.

Acceptance is not the same as detachment

The Shaolin principle teaches us that being detached does not mean that we must forego things. It is not a barter, not a sacrifice to obtain something else in return. It is essentially a change in wanting.

Living by the principle means to accept things as they are and genuinely not wish for them to be otherwise. It means accepting what comes and goes with equanimity as also winning and losing.

The principle of detachment teaches us to do things because we want to do them, not because we want to gain something in return.

It serves as a defence, not as an attack technique. Someone who has truly mastered this principle is unassailable for most opponents. So, the next time you greet someone, have absolutely no expectations.

EXERCISES

SHEDDING THE THINGS THAT WEIGH YOU DOWN

The following questions should give you an idea of how rich you really are and how the desire to possess makes you vulnerable.

What does a friend mean to you?

....

Which are the three things you would take with you to a remote island?

....

Which three persons would you take along?

....

And finally, which three talents would you take?

....

If all of a sudden, absolutely everything you owned was stolen, what would be your first wish?

....

Who has power over you because they are in a position to give you something?

....

Why have you given this person this power?

....

Part Two

Learn to Be Strong

Any man who tries to be good all the time is bound to come to ruin among the great number who are not good. Hence, he must learn how not to be good, and use that knowledge, or refrain from using it, as necessity requires.

Niccolò Machiavelli

Smile, and forget it.

Chinese proverb

5. The Principle of Calmness

Calmness is the graceful form of confidence.

Marie von Ebner-Eschenbach

Learn, never to get carried away into doing anything.

A young Zen monk, so the story goes in Shaolin, was entrusted with delivering an important letter. On his way he had to cross a bridge, but when he reached there, he found an experienced samurai blocking his path. This samurai had taken a vow to challenge the first hundred men crossing the bridge to a duel. He had already killed ninety-nine. The monk entreated the samurai to let him pass since he had a very important letter to deliver. He promised he would return to duel with the samurai as soon as he had delivered the letter. The samurai hesitated at first but then agreed and the monk was able to resume his journey.

Once he had delivered the letter and certain that he would die soon, the monk sought out his master to bid him farewell.

'I must fight with a great samurai, and I have never even held a sword. He will certainly kill me.'

'Indeed,' the master replied, 'you will die because you have no chance of winning. So, I will teach you the best way to die: raise your sword above your head, keep your eyes firmly shut and wait. When you feel something cold on the top of your head, that is death. At that moment, let your arms drop, along with everything you believe you possess. That is all.'

The unequal combat

The monk bowed before his master and returned to the bridge where the samurai awaited him. The two prepared for combat.

The monk did exactly what his master had advised him to do. He took his sword in both hands, raised it above his head, closed his eyes and waited, absolutely motionless. This greatly surprised and confused the samurai because his opponent's bearing betrayed no fear whatsoever. Growing suspicious, he cautiously approached the monk, who stood there calmly, concentrating only on the top of his head.

The samurai thought, 'This man is obviously extremely strong. He had the courage to return and fight me.' The monk continued to stand there motionless. The samurai grew increasingly confused and, all of a sudden, he was certain: 'This man, without doubt, is an exceptional warrior. He adopts an attacking stance from the start and then closes his eyes!' The monk had meanwhile completely forgotten the samurai. He was focused so completely on following the advice of his master and dying with dignity that he stood there detached and free of all worldly concerns. By now the samurai was convinced that he would be sliced in two were he to make the slightest move. In a pleading tone he finally began to speak: 'I beseech you, have pity and do not kill me. I considered myself to be a master of swordplay but I know now that I have met a true master today. Please accept me as your student and teach me the way of swordsmanship.'

Calmness is a weapon

You might be thinking, how could a monk who did nothing but stand and wait for his death be a good teacher of swordsmanship? You might also wonder why, after having urged you to action in the last four chapters, I am now telling you this story.

Isn't the monk doing exactly what we should *not* be doing, that is, doing nothing and waiting? Should he not have charged at the samurai with absolute determination and at least tried to save his life in combat? No. In this case that would have meant certain death.

Let us go over the story again. A Zen monk who has never held a sword is facing an experienced master swordsman. He cannot win a conventional combat under any circumstances. His master advises him to stay calm. 'Do not fear and do not do anything.' He follows this advice and it is this calmness, the act of doing nothing that leads the samurai to a wrong conclusion, which ultimately saves the monk's life. Simply by switching positions he forces the samurai to act. It is incorrect to think that the monk did nothing and therefore won.

The Shaolin principle of calmness teaches us that conscious inaction can be an effective means of defence—if we employ it with the right resolve.

The art of self-control

True calmness is an ability that most people lose during the course of their lives. Many of us start reacting before we have even fully comprehended a situation, perhaps out of anger, habit or being over-conscientious. Lack of inner calmness makes you predictable. You might have heard that Asian martial arts exponents employ their opponent's own strength against them.

Your calmness can be a very powerful weapon, especially in situations where the opponent is agitated or enraged.

'When you are unable to discern what is in the mind of your opponent…feint an attack and his mind will then be reflected in the movement of his sword,' writes Musashi.

A feint in this case does not mean an attack but a swift movement in the opponent's direction. A bluff in other words. If an opponent is truly calm and responds according to the demands of the situation, not some plan they decided in advance, there would be nothing they could divulge. A lunge at the opponent, after all, is not an actual attack and doesn't call for any kind of reaction. The opponent could continue standing motionless and coolly observe that you have obviously not divined their intentions. Armed with this knowledge they could then themselves act. In real life, however, the situation would be the other way round. Your opponent has a plan and is merely waiting for a signal or a reason to execute it. If the situation were to change, they would no longer be able to adapt their actions since they would be too focused on what they were planning to do.

Luring opponents into dropping their guard

Deceptive moves—I call them 'mock attacks'—are a well-known tactic in Shaolin kung fu and don't merely involve feigning a strike. They are meant to entice the opponent into dropping their guard and provoke them into making a mistake.

Let us assume that the attacker plans to punch the opponent's chest with their right fist. If they do so directly, the opponent will easily spot their intention and parry the blow. The attacker must therefore disturb the opponent's poise.

With the left hand the attacker delivers a very light jab to the opponent's head. The opponent loses their cool and reacts by trying to block the high blow. In doing so they expose their chest. The attacker's hard punch that follows is delivered precisely at this spot. Naturally, this technique is not restricted to boxing.

Someone who is forced into (re)acting emotionally while defending almost always loses.

Defensive moves that are emotionally motivated cloud the ability to discern the true intentions of the attacker.

Good fighters employ the technique of 'mock attacks' wherever possible. They force their opponents into situations where they get emotional about defending themselves and thus lose their calm.

Let's say, I want to know where you were last evening but you don't want to tell me. You would recognise a direct question and immediately block it, so I would invent something to accuse you of. I could claim, for instance, that you damaged someone's car at a random location. I would say very calmly, 'It doesn't really concern me, but some witnesses claim that your car banged into another car.'

You would insist that it wasn't you and the ensuing discussion would get increasingly heated.

'Who else could it have been? You're obviously a bad driver.'

'No, I'm not.'

'Of course you are. Otherwise it wouldn't have happened.'

This would go on until you finally let the cat out of the bag that it definitely wasn't you because you were with XY the whole evening, and since they lived so close by you didn't take the car out at all. 'Oh, so you were with XY?' I would have won that round. The car would be irrelevant.

Every feint is based on the opponent losing their nerve and judging before knowing all the facts. Even if you had actually caused some damage with your car, it would be none of my business. Had you remained calm and not reacted to my mock attack, you would have said, 'Then let that person file a complaint. I know it wasn't me.' And I would have got no information out of you.

A bus driver told me how once he had to stop his bus going uphill on a very steep road. When starting off again, the bus slid back a little and, to his horror, the driver heard the sound of crunching glass. He looked in his rear-view mirror and saw a Mercedes with a shattered indicator light and damaged bumper. He got out and walked over to the damaged car wondering how he would explain the blunder. As he was launching into an apology, in that split second before he could open his mouth, the driver of the Mercedes said, 'I'm terribly sorry. I wanted to start off on the slope but my foot slipped off the clutch and I rammed into your bus…'

Giving up before the fight

An over-conscientious attitude also reveals a lack of calmness, and it can often land people in serious trouble. Imagine that you are on a train and the conductor is approaching your seat. He is actually in a hurry and has no interest in checking your ticket because the train is approaching the final station. You, however, start rummaging in your pockets to show him your monthly pass. Suddenly, you realise that you forgot it at home. But since you have drawn the conductor's attention he stops, asks to see your ticket and collects a hefty fine. Had you remained composed, the conductor would have passed by and you would have saved yourself an expensive lesson—because you were not really travelling ticketless.

Weaponising your opponent's fear

Really good fighters are able to exploit a lack of calmness far more than that. They don't even have to do much. They simply leverage their opponents' fears. Of course, fear is sometimes important, but in most cases, it is your biggest enemy.

Let us go back to our train. This time let us assume that

you knew you left your monthly pass at home. If you did not know this, you could calmly observe the conductor coming and going and he would see you calmly sitting in your seat. Now, however, he will notice your nervousness and sense that you have something to hide. The logical consequence would be a friendly, 'May I see your ticket please…?'

As far as fear is concerned, we humans are very similar to animals: we can literally smell it. A mighty elephant allows itself to be controlled by a tiny human as long as this person displays no fear. But if the same person shows they are scared to a little dog, the animal suddenly becomes loud, aggressive and dangerous. It is a similar situation with people who threaten they will complain to a superior at the slightest pretext. What such people want to hear is a fearful, 'Please don't!' That lets them know they have gained power over their opponent and they will certainly follow through on their threat so as to strengthen their own position.

What would happen if, instead, the response was, 'That's a great idea! I was just speaking with my boss yesterday about people who feel they are nobodies if they don't threaten others. You have the boss's email address, don't you?' It's irrelevant whether your boss is actually as easy-going as that. The mail will never be sent.

If you can control your fear of your opponent, you have already won half the battle.

'It is important to know the enemy's sword…' Do you remember? Those who allow themselves to be distracted by its movements, or worse still, to react to them, can easily be manipulated and consequently defeated.

EXERCISES

HOW EASILY CAN YOU BE MANIPULATED?

I will now demonstrate how even you can be manipulated into doing what you believe is expected of you. Please concentrate fully on the following task and do not read further until you have solved it. Even if you already know this puzzle or do not like maths, please complete it. The solution is given below so please don't peek. Ready? Good.

The bus ride: Seven passengers are sitting on a bus. At the first stop four passengers get off and three board the bus. At the next stop no one gets off and two people get on, then three get off and eight get on. Are you keeping track? The bus drives on to the next stop where nine passengers get on and four get off. One stop later two get off and five get on. At the next stop six passengers leave the bus. It reaches its final destination and all the passengers get off.

Can you now tell me how often the bus stopped?

Probably not. After all, you assumed that you would be asked about the number of passengers remaining on the bus, didn't you? But my question could have been about anything, e.g.: what you had for lunch yesterday or what your favourite colour is. Either way, I would have achieved my objective.

I wrote nothing that in any way suggested you keep count, but you did. With that I diverted your attention from other things. Had you been calm, you would have heard or read the entire question before taking any action.

- Please reflect: Why did you start counting? What would have happened if you had not? What were you afraid of?
- Please write down three situations in which you reacted similarly, and three in which this could happen to you.

People who aren't calm are even more vulnerable. One can, of course, disturb their concentration and distract them, but one can also provoke them into action. Here is an example: read each question below and give the first answer that comes to your mind before moving on to the next. Please say your answers out loud and clear. I am going to try and make you say 'blue' without your wanting to. Let's start:

- What is the colour of grass?

- What is the colour of the sun?
- What colour is your skin?
- What is the colour of roses?
- What colour are dandelions?
- What colour is soil?

Did you answer 'brown'? That was what I expected, I told you that you would say 'brown' without wanting to.

Did you now think, it wasn't 'brown', it was 'blue' you weren't going to say? So at least I was able to make you think 'blue'. And if I was sitting in front of you, you would have said it.

Provoke your opponents and they will reveal themselves and their intentions. Strip them of their composure and they will do things they actually do not want to do.

As they say in Shaolin, a good fighter has no anger. Nor should they. After all, when is it easiest to get carried away into doing or saying something that you will later really regret? When do you have the least inhibitions about giving your boss, partner or whoever a proper piece of your mind, saying hurtful things that you don't actually mean, but which then linger on forever? When do you jeopardise most of the opportunities in your life in the shortest possible time? When do you gift a calm opponent the best openings to turn your own strengths against you? When you are well and truly angry. When you are blind with rage, as the saying puts it so well. Of course, anger and rage can be necessary for survival in some situations. Sometimes they can even serve to emphasise determination. But it's best to fight without them.

A furious person has power.
But they have no control over the situation or the consequences of their actions.

If you hurl something at the wall in rage, it breaks. It doesn't matter how much you may regret it later. Things said can also never be made unsaid. Besides, anger only saps our own energy and works against us.

You probably know the following situation only too well. You are driving your car on a narrow road, when suddenly the driver in the car alongside recklessly cuts you off. Fortunately, nothing happens, but it could have ended badly. You immediately start cursing the idiot and get so agitated that you almost drive into the ditch. Once you are a little calmer, you ask your co-passenger if they noted the licence plate number, which you forgot because you were so busy cursing.

Naturally they didn't. In a flash, your anger returns, but this time it is directed at the innocent passenger. After some time, you realise that your behaviour was inappropriate and apologise but justify it with the reproach that they should have applied their mind. And bang, your anger is back.

Your anger harms only you

What did you achieve? The lout you were cursing is probably already sitting somewhere with friends, having a beer. He is fine because he isn't even aware of your anger. Your passenger pities you for being so aggressive and turns to the window to enjoy the passing scenery.

And you? You will have realised that anger is always directed only against oneself. In this case against yourself because you are the only one who is not happy. You might now say, 'If I were to stay calm then that idiot would continue driving badly until at some point something serious happens!'

But what did your cursing achieve, except that you don't even know his licence plate number? And that you yourself are not happy?

It is a similar situation when the last bus for the day drives off before your very eyes. You could curse the bus driver, the bus company, the city or even life in general. The people standing around will only smile in pity. No one else will even know—neither the bus driver nor the CEO of the bus company. But you would have wasted many minutes of your own life.

'If you are agitated,' they say in Shaolin, 'do and say nothing. Slowly breathe in and breathe out and wait till your spirit is calm and clear once more.'

A wise person once told me that each of us is responsible for how we feel. That applies to you too. While anger may, on occasion, be quite justified, you must always be conscious of what you are actually angry about. Do you want to scream to let off steam or to change something? Screaming does not help to achieve lasting change. A furious soldier just thrashes about wildly.

The principle of calmness teaches us to convert our opponents' anger and fear to our advantage. It teaches us to remain calm even in the bleakest situations and to not let ourselves get carried away. The next time someone challenges you and you feel you might lose control, simply smile. And then forget it.

EXERCISES

CALMNESS CAN BE LEARNT

One can learn calmness. After all, anger is just in your head. I will show you how it works.

- The next time you almost burst a blood vessel with fury or when fear makes you think you must act immediately, concentrate on your breathing. Gift yourself ten moments. You will not miss out on anything during this time. Slowly breathe in and then breathe out.

- You might have the urge to charge off and take some action at once, but control this urge. Bang on the imaginary table, think 'stop it' and continue to breathe calmly.
- Now consciously start sensing your body (see page 34). Do you feel how the anger drains out as you become calmer?

'You are right, of course, but...' And once again we are back where we started. Yet again, emotion trumps intellect. If you are one of those people who find it hard to stop and whose anger keeps reigniting, then you must expand your defence technique.

- Think of any random word. It should be something that you are often reminded of, for example the word 'hand'.
- From now on, this word is your 'stop word'. It means that whenever you hear this word or think of it in a situation where you are not able to control your feelings or actions, you must immediately stop talking and suppress any 'yes, but...,' or 'but I still think that...'. Just stop and say to yourself, 'Even if I have a different opinion it doesn't matter. I will simply stop talking.'
- Breathe slowly until you feel the urge has passed.

With a bit of practice you will manage this without anyone noticing.

EXERCISES

DRAWING STRENGTH FROM CALMNESS

Are you aware of the weapons that opponents can use against you? And do you know which weapons you have for defence?

What is your 'stop word'?

....

Write down five things that can make you really angry.

....

In which situation did you most recently get carried away?

....

What were the consequences of your actions?

....

When was the last time you were at a disadvantage because you were over-conscientious?

....

When did a situation turn out differently after you had already taken action?

....

Has fear ever got you into a needlessly unpleasant situation?

....

If you are in a hurry, walk slowly.

Chinese proverb

6. The Principle of Slowness

Overshooting the mark is just
as bad as falling short of it.

Confucius

Learn to conquer haste with slowness

When my great grandfather described his first day at school in the year 1896, he recounted a 'good-natured grey horse pulling our carriage'. A fascinating picture forms in the reader's mind: the child along with his father slowly and serenely approaches the big city, which he has never seen. They pass the city walls, cross through the town, which is actually more like a village and, after a two-hour ride, they finally reach the school.

In a modern-day car, both of them would probably have covered the distance in ten minutes. For the older generation, whose life spanned a large part of the previous century, the most enduring impression of change is probably the unbelievable surge in speed. All of a sudden, the horse-drawn carriage and the leisureliness associated with it are a thing of the past.

As early as the second century CE, the Romans used horse-drawn chariots for warfare. Increasing the number of horses harnessed to this vehicle made it possible to increase its capacity, but not the speed. Even the strongest chariot could not move faster than the horses could run.

For 1800 years, the manageable pace of the chariot was considered the benchmark since it was simply impossible to go faster. Only when it was discovered that higher speed was a money-spinner did things begin to change rapidly. In place of the leisurely carriage came the car, express train, aeroplane, and supersonic plane. It was all about speed: ideally one would be back even before starting! There is a famous rule in computer engineering by Gordon Moore, who predicted in 1965 that microprocessor speeds would double about every eighteen months. In simple terms this means that every 1.5 years, computers become twice as fast as the preceding generation of computers. So, in fifteen years, computers will be a thousand times faster than they are today.

Fast-paced life

Speed has become the magic mantra of our times. Reading faster, learning faster, eating faster… dashing off on a quick holiday, returning home even quicker. Essentially, we are living life at a faster pace.

But then what? Take the speeding up of communication in recent years. Earlier, a letter would take at least two days in one direction and two days for the return post. Faxes were faster. You would write and print the letter, stick it in the fax machine and dial the number. Too slow? Fine, email became the answer. Now you simply click on 'reply' and the message reaches the recipient immediately. Computers have simplified our lives and made our work quicker and thereby more efficient. One can now do the same work in half the time, or make double the money in the same time. So objectively, the enhancement in speed is something good. The question is, now that you are able to complete your work in half the time do you actually have more leisure time as a result? Or to put it differently:

What have you gained by the increase in speed? And what has it cost you?

Please make three columns in your notebook.

In the first column, please note down the personal advantages you achieve from the general escalation in speed.

In the second column, please write down what you would consider to be the disadvantages. Leave the third column blank for now. Attempt to find concrete things, such as more time to chat with your friends and family, extra time for yourself, greater financial independence. However, if you think, for example, that greater speeds now allow you to reach holiday destinations more quickly, please consider carefully how exactly this benefits you personally. Is it not possible to enjoy the journey to the destination?

Now for the third column. Against every entry in the disadvantages column, please now note who, in your opinion, benefits from the faster pace. For instance, if in the second column you wrote, 'I have to put in even more overtime now because customers expect that their orders will be dispatched on the same day,' in the third column you could note that the company now makes more profits. The owners would be the beneficiaries.

'There is more to life than increasing its speed,' Mahatma Gandhi once said. In our speed-dominated society, however, slowness is considered uncool. Stillness tends to be equated with laziness. Someone not rushing from one appointment to the next evidently has nothing to do. Mobile phones help you make productive use of supposedly wasted travel time, during which in earlier days you would simply have switched off. 'Just very quickly' doing something has become the buzzword of our times.

If life is a mad rush, is stillness considered death? There are actually more examples of people dying from driving too fast, from heart attacks caused by excessive stress or a distracted misstep, than those for whom their stillness became their undoing.

Don't allow yourself to be rushed!

In the hands of an experienced warrior, speed is a dangerous weapon. If an offer is on sale 'only until tomorrow', you are likely to grab it without much thought. On the other hand, if the same product is 'on permanent discount', you will wait and think it through. You might then realise that you don't actually need the apparent bargain. Your slowness is clearly not in the interest of your opponent. Once again, the IT industry presents a very interesting case study. 'Don't miss this offer: superfast computer available for the next three days only at this extraordinary, one-time, special price! (The original sales price will apply after the offer expires).' What is noteworthy about this example? In this case, your opponent is very obviously pushing you to take a decision that you will later regret. If you were to take a step back, it would be clear to you that this supposed 'offer' can't be one. Computers, as we noted above, are becoming more efficient and powerful by the day, as their prices keep dropping. Then how could a computer which is going to become outdated in a few days anyway suddenly become more expensive once the sale is over?

When a waiter at a restaurant wants to take your order for drinks before you have even taken off your jacket, it may well be with the same intention. Without having had a look at the drinks menu, you might order something that is exorbitantly priced.

Haste leads to mistakes

Since the speed principle, however, is so firmly entrenched in our thinking, most people find it difficult to recognise the opponent's true intentions. Someone who is asked to 'just quickly sign this' is about to walk into a trap. Similar to driving, the probability of making mistakes and losing control increases in direct proportion to the speed. It may sound morbid, but even in the automobile sector, speed is in the interest of the manufacturer. Every wrecked car creates an opportunity to sell a new one.

> Find five examples in which an opponent has the upper hand by making you hurry. Write these down in your notebook.

Bad buys, bad decisions or blunders: the Shaolin principle teaches us that haste leads to mistakes and that rushing prevents us from seeing the big picture. It teaches us that someone who can push us into rushing already has the upper hand.

Causing someone to hurry, means provoking them into making mistakes.

Over the years, the Shaolin monks have developed weapons that are carried discreetly, without being spotted by the opponent. It is the same with being made to rush. Follow me briefly into a clothing store. You ask to be shown different outfits, you try a few but are not really bowled over by anything. What could the salesperson now do to push you into making a purchase? They will let you know that their time is limited. One way is by calling out several times to a customer who is just browsing, 'I'll be with you in just a minute!'

Many people become nervous because of this kind of behaviour and think, 'I've taken up so much of the salesperson's time, let me just buy something. It's not so bad after all.'

What is overlooked in this situation (and why you finally also lose the battle with the salesperson) is that they are employed to spend a certain part of their day on the shop floor. They are paid to come in at nine in the morning and remain until six in the evening. So, whether they work or not, they have to stay in that shop for nine hours. If the salesperson deals with all twelve customers coming in on a day within two hours, they will have to stand around for seven hours. It makes no difference to their free time. Consequently, if the salesperson tries to rush you into deciding, it has nothing to do with their time. But what they manage to do is to push you into buying something that you originally never intended to.

Slowness is a principle of nature

Being able to slow down is one of our most important abilities which, like so many other things, we seem to have lost over the years. If you have ever observed dogs on their morning walks you would have noticed that slowness is a principle of nature. If there were no human escort tugging and pushing and finally carrying them, the animal itself would have all the time in the world. And why not? If it were to adopt the pace of their human and simply run past everything without really perceiving it, what would it gain? Even evolution doesn't mean change on an hourly basis. Good things take their time, and nature thinks in dimensions of millennia, if not millions of years.

You want a stone that is polished absolutely smooth?
Place it in a stream and come back after fifty years.
Then it might be ready.

A Chinese proverb says, 'If you must hurry, then hurry slowly.' This might sound paradoxical but it is not, because walking slowly lets you arrive faster.

EXERCISES

SLOW IS FASTER

I will once again give you an example. I'm sure you have a watch somewhere that lets you count seconds. You also need your notebook.

- In the next paragraph you will find ten nonsense words. Your task is to order them alphabetically as quickly as possible. When your stopwatch is ready you can start.
- As soon as you have finished, you must check the result and only then write down how long you took. You should be able to solve the exercise in twenty seconds.
- Please read on only after you have completed the exercise.
- Here are the words: avariec, avric, aivrce, avarice, aavirec, avrice, airvec, avirace, aavrice, averic.

Finished? Of course you took longer than twenty seconds. It would be impossible to finish in that amount of time. I only wanted to make you hurry. Perhaps you started quickly but then you must have had to make some corrections – and that is what takes time.

Let us try the same exercise again. But this time do not do it as quickly as possible, make sure that you need to correct as little as possible.

- When the clock starts, first think of a way to approach the task and then stick to that method. Don't forget: it's not speed but accuracy that counts.
- Your words for this exercise are: bflido, bolfiold, bolflid, blodfli, blodlif, bolfid, bofioldo, bofdli, bfloido, bofoildo.
- How long did you take this time? And more importantly, did you make fewer mistakes?

Whenever you get into a situation where you start thinking frantically, remind yourself of the principle of slowness. You might have experienced situations where in your hurry you weren't able to insert a key in the lock or knot a necktie. At such times force yourself to slow down. You will see that it works wonders.

Speed can be a tactic

The principle of calmness taught us not to give an answer before we are asked. The principle of slowness goes a step further. If we know only the beginning of the answer to a question, it makes sense to answer so slowly that the person asking is no longer interested in hearing the end.

When I appeared for my school-leaving oral examination in maths many years ago, I was faced with exactly this problem.

I knew how to start answering most questions but at some point, I would get stuck. My maths teacher was aware of this.

I wanted to impress the examiners by showing how quick I was in solving the questions. My strategy was that once the examiners saw how fast I began they would assume that I could solve that question and ask me to move on to the next. I worked as if my life depended on it. My teacher tried to slow down my pace with a calm, 'Very good. Now do this…'

As soon as I felt somewhat certain about one section, I worked even faster. After I failed the exam because naturally, my deficiencies had been exposed, my maths teacher taught me a life-long lesson. I can still hear his words today: 'You are dumb. You knew that there is a fixed time allotted for each candidate to be tested by the panel of examiners, after which the exam has to conclude. I knew that you wouldn't be able to solve the sums after a point, so I kept telling you, first do this. If you had worked slowly, the time would have been up and I would have said, "You obviously know the rest, right?" But you worked so fast that at the end everyone could see you were stuck.'

Try and find three examples where slowness can be superior to speed and write them down in your notebook.

Another characteristic of speed is that after a point it takes on a life of its own. Trying to do more and more, faster and faster, will lead to a point where fatigue causes slowing down. This can only be offset by adopting an even faster method of working, which then leads to more mistakes and a decline in overall productivity. In such a situation, if you were to propose to the person who is working to take a break, you would usually get a perplexed response. How can one even think of a break when there is so much work to be done? The deadline is looming! Actually, the time to take a break is precisely when there is no time to take a break.

Girl and boy scouts employ a technique they call the 'scout stride' to reach their destination as quickly as possible. The idea is *not* to walk as fast as you can until you drop. Instead, keep slowing down from time to time. For example, first run 200 strides, then walk the same distance, then run again, and so on. If needed, this can be kept up for hours without break. If you don't confuse slowness with dawdling, and doing nothing with laziness, you will discover to your surprise the fast pace that stillness enables.

'It is better to do nothing than to achieve nothing with a lot of effort,' said Lao Tzu.

Earlier we learnt that one can provoke other people into making mistakes by rushing them. And yet, many people continue to believe that they must master everything on priority as quickly as possible.

Whether it is playing the piano, learning magic tricks or

training in martial arts—people tend to think that errors can be covered up through speed. It seems that the main goal of practice no longer is to execute as perfectly, but as quickly as possible. In fact, for a martial arts technique like Shaolin kung fu, where even the position of individual fingers has significance, this approach would be disastrous. Too many important details would be overlooked. Novices at the Shaolin temple are told that if you can do something quickly it does not mean that you can also do it slowly. To be able to do something swiftly, you must begin by learning to do it very slowly. You must keep forcing yourself to slow down. Swiftness will then come automatically. Everything that you master slowly, you will, over time, also be able to execute faster. In an age that is so dominated by speed, there is a fascination for 'slow living'.

Rediscover your own pace

We don't want to watch a warrior monk's attacking moves with a sword at a 5x timelapse; we want to see each move in slow motion. The Shaolin principle teaches us that slowness and stillness are very powerful weapons. We are inclined to believe someone speaking slowly and calmly rather than someone agitatedly defending themselves, irrespective of who is actually telling the truth.

Yet, many people today regard slowness as an unattainable privilege. I often get to hear, 'I wish I had your calmness.'

'I would gladly give it to you,' I then think, 'but you don't really want to have it.' Remember, whoever controls your pace also controls your life. And that, I hope, will once again soon be you.

EXERCISES

SLOW DOWN YOUR PACE

Before slowing down, one must know what one's true pace is. The questions below will help you find out.

What makes you feel really rushed?

....

How much time do you take for your meals per day, and how much time would you like to have?

....

Where would you have reached faster if you had 'gone slower'?

....

Where did your fast pace result in errors being exposed that would otherwise have gone unnoticed?

....

If the pace of everything were to go back to what it was 100 years ago, how would that be a disadvantage to you, and what would the advantages be?

....

What is happening too fast in your life?

....

What can you do to apply the brakes?

....

The wise man learns from his mistakes; the wiser man learns from the mistakes of others.

Confucius

7. The Principle of Imitation

Those who are small must know well those who are large, and those who are large must know those who are small.

Miyamoto Musashi

Learn, that you can gauge people better by imitating them.

When Bodhidharma and the monks with him founded the Shaolin monastery on Hao-shan Mountain over 1500 years ago, they had to deal with two main challenges.

One, the area around the monastery was unsafe due to the presence of robbers and vagabonds. These elements could be managed over time, but the much more dangerous problem facing them was that of the wild animals roaming the forests because they were unpredictable. How could this danger be overcome? Good warriors can defend themselves against people. But how to do so against an animal?

The first residents of the monastery thought of a solution that was as simple as it was brilliant: Why not employ the same methods of defence that animals use when attacked by other animals? Why not simply observe the animals and beat them with their own techniques? The monks began to analyse and finally to copy the behaviour of their wild adversaries and, suddenly, they were in a position to defeat their supposedly superior opponents.

Humans like to regard themselves as the 'pinnacle of creation', although strictly speaking they have not been given many abilities. They are neither particularly big nor strong, nor really robust and also not very fast. What distinguishes humans from other living beings is their ability to deliberately imitate. This has helped them survive till today.

The ability to identify the strengths of animals and to combine these with human intellect have given us a certain superiority in many situations.

The monk and the mantis

In the Shaolin monastery, the monk Wang Lang was regarded as an experienced warrior who had mastered seventeen kung fu styles. But despite the most rigorous training, he was unable to defeat his fellow monks in duels. Crestfallen, he withdrew to a nearby forest. One day, during a walk, he observed a fight between a praying mantis and a cicada, during which the little praying mantis managed to defeat the cicada many times its size.

Wang Lang was impressed. He caught the praying mantis and began to observe it. For weeks he studied its movements and began to develop a completely new fighting style. Since the praying mantis fights mainly with its 'arms', Wang Lang incorporated the mantis's hand techniques into his style. He then adopted leg techniques from the style of monkeys, and finally he added the best elements from other martial arts styles that were known to him.

He took his time developing and carefully honing the new technique and only then did he return to the monastery. There he was able to defeat a large number of monks in a friendly contest. The abbot was thrilled and the style was officially included in the Shaolin library. Students copied it from their masters and in turn taught the same to their own students.

The 'praying mantis' style has been one of the most important Shaolin kung fu techniques for almost 400 years.

Learning through imitation

It is not just martial arts that have been inspired by imitating nature. The principle of imitation is as old as life itself. It might have negative connotations in our society but without imitation nature would no longer exist.

No young animal would know how to hunt or be in the position to teach itself. It mimics the centuries-old techniques that it picks up from its mother. Swimming, climbing, fighting… no animal reinvents something that already exists. It will pick up anything that helps it to survive. It's better to improve something that exists than to invent it a second time.

The Shaolin monks also embraced this principle. Why develop your own fighting techniques when the best already exists? It is better to channel one's energy into observing and adapting.

The Greek philosopher Aristotle observed that everything that depends on the action of nature is by nature as good as it can be.

The human voice serves as the reference pitch for instruments. The eye can see more colours than any technical device in the world can capture. The computing power of the brain makes supercomputers pale in comparison. No human being, no matter how wise, can ever create anything better.

Consequently, whatever humans have supposedly invented are merely poor imitations. Take the wheel, flying, or artificial intelligence: everything can be found in a far superior form in nature and has only been copied by humans. Which is not really a problem, is it? An old proverb says that a good imitation is better than a bad invention.

And yet, this is precisely what is often frowned upon. People invest hundreds and thousands of hours into reinventing something that already exists. Just for the fame, just to be able to say later, 'I invented that myself!'

I sometimes ask myself, what would have happened to the Shaolin kung fu techniques and all the other combat styles if the monks in Shaolin had thought like this? What if each of them had started developing their techniques from scratch instead of adapting what was already known? It goes without saying that other people's ideas should only serve as a starting point for one's own. It is most certainly in bad taste to rest on someone else's laurels or products, but that is not what this is about.

Please take your notebook again and write down five things that you wanted to invent by yourself even though you could have achieved the same outcome faster by imitation. It might have been the best possible route for a trip, which you didn't want to ask for advice about. Or maybe you didn't want to ask someone to explain a simpler way of using a device. Also write down what prevented you from simplifying the process through imitation.

Have you ever thought about how a child learns? They do so by imitating the behaviour of their caregivers. Children copy the successful behavioural patterns of others to achieve a certain objective. If they want attention, affection or food, they try to imitate as closely as possible the words that they have heard adults use in the same situation.

Imitation and role models

If a child were to think of imitation as something negative and invent its own language, we could soon forget about communication. But it's not only language that children imitate. Just as young animals mimic the hunting behaviour of their parents, humans tend to copy the behaviour of those whom they look up to. If a successful businessman wears a suit and tie, we also wear the same to project a successful image. Indeed, fashion as a concept and the money it generates are also based on imitation. Someone or the other wears a particular style, so it's considered modern. Someone is non-conformist and wants to express their individuality by shaving their head, so all others who want to be recognised as individuals will shave their heads too. While it is often not considered very classy, the need to imitate is rooted deep within us.

Powerful sales method

One of the classic weapons of modern sales and advertising is based on this knowledge. It is very effective because it is usually concealed. On television we learn that the successful celebrity X has their funds managed by Bank A, uses a mobile connection by Provider B and drives a Brand C car. Another well-known personality Y, it is said, also swears by the same combination. No one claims that X or Y are successful because they use these products. Who would know if X privately thinks that Bank A provides terrible service?

However, the sword that was thus far concealed has now been drawn. Who doesn't wish to be successful? The victim's mind starts ticking over: both these personalities must have a reason to swear by these specific products. There's a reason they are successful, so even if these are not the only factors, there has to be a connection. And, in fact, friend D also has an account with the same bank and is very satisfied.

Ultimately, recommendations are the bedrock of imitation. If O goes somewhere and is satisfied, then I must check it out. If P and Q are happy with brand Z, let me try it out too.

Opinion leaders

In advertising jargon, people who are imitated by many other people are called opinion leaders. The advertising industry has realised how important it is to co-opt such people as partners, be they journalists, course instructors, authors, doctors, etc. The opinions of such people are usually unquestioningly accepted. Even if it turns out at some point that opinion leaders can make mistakes or, perhaps, they were not entirely selfless in their advice, we still assume the fault must lie with us. As children we learnt to imitate adults in order to survive. Later in life many people continue to find it hard to live without copying another person.

> Please write in your notebook who has influenced you and also who views you as an opinion leader. Find three people or institutions each for both cases, and note down alongside who imitates whom and why.

If you apply the principle of imitation correctly, you can unleash its full power. For one, it helps us avoid committing those mistakes that others have already made. And second, getting into the mind of an opponent gives us deep insights into their thinking and actions.

Someone who imitates others can avoid repeating their mistakes. The fighting technique used by monkeys was certainly not perfect from the very first day, and over time it must have cost several monkeys their lives. Perhaps there is even something that can be improved upon in the fighting style of the praying mantis. By using its hind legs more skilfully it may be able to win more fights. It is precisely these—possibly fatal—mistakes in combat that can be identified by observation and avoided through imitation. However, since no mantis will ever think of copying the monkey's leg technique and must develop everything by itself, humans are superior in this respect. My point is that while being imitated can sometimes be annoying, it certainly also has positive aspects.

Confucius said that there are three methods by which we may learn wisdom: first, by reflection, which is the noblest; second, by imitation, which is the easiest; and third, by experience, which is the bitterest.

If you decide to write a book similar to this one, I would not be able to stop you. Why should I even try? You will never be able to ensure that it is identical, so perhaps I might even learn something from your book. For instance, the examples you provide might be better ones that I had not considered, and which I could then include in the next edition of my book. Consequently, it would present a distinct advantage for me to be copied.

A big fear among many people is that imitation might result in something being taken away from them. For example, you could take my topic and attempt to write a very similar book. Please do so. Even if you now know the entire contents, your book will never be the same as mine. There is no reason for me to be afraid, and certainly not because of the argument that 'something similar already exists'. That doesn't count. If things were really to function like that then we would have exactly one clothing company that would produce just one model of a suit, shirt and trouser.

There would be only one type of computer, music system and kitchen gadget.

For many years the Japanese followed the principle of 'copy and improve'. The success of companies like Sony, Yamaha and Canon proves them right. I would nevertheless not be afraid because my book cannot be copied. I recall what a photographer colleague once said when talking about sharing lighting techniques, 'Even if I were to tell you exactly where I placed my lights and fixed your camera settings, you would never be able to compose my picture.' But in the process he might get some ideas about what he could do better the next time.

Reflect on what is worth imitating

All the same, mindless imitation can also be counterproductive, and not merely because our opponents can use it against us. As I wrote above, the idea of learning is based on copying. It is nevertheless imperative to reflect in advance about what is worth imitating. Many of us have got so used to accepting authority that we no longer question before acting. But consider that if everyone were simply to reproduce what they learn from their teachers, no development would occur. The German satirist Kurt Tucholsky summed it up very aptly, 'Don't be impressed by an expert who tells you, "Dear friend, I have been doing it this way for twenty years!"—One can also do something wrong for twenty years.' Imitation without reflection stifles opportunities for change. Everyone in a country might be disgusted with the current state of politics, but because their parents and grandparents voted for party P, they unthinkingly do the same.

Do you also imitate things out of sheer habit, without questioning why? Write down five such things in your notebook.

On the other hand, flawless imitation of a person or thing can lead an opponent to draw wrong conclusions. Nature has perfected this idea in the form of camouflage. But we also happily believe in the clumsiness of a clown on stage who stumbles over everything. The Shaolin monks used this knowledge to develop a method to deceive opponents. They would pretend to be heavily drunk and mimic the movements of an inebriated person so accurately that opponents would be misled into believing they were dealing with a defenceless victim. In earlier times, this often proved to be a deadly mistake.

The Shaolin principle teaches us that successful imitation must fulfil two requirements: it must be carried out without any value judgement and it must be exhaustive. The following example should illustrate this. An actor playing the role of a villain must *become* the character with their entire being.

They must walk evil, talk evil, eat evil, think evil. Even if they reject all this in their actual lives, they must leave their ideas of morality in the changing room. In their role they are truly evil, otherwise they would not embody a villain but only come across as someone playing one.

'When you imitate a monkey, then with your whole body, heart and mind you must become a monkey,' one learns in Shaolin. In the practice of Zen meditation this technique of being able to get into someone else's skin also allows you to achieve the emptiness of mind that paves the way to enlightenment. When you are concentrating on being a dragon there is no place in your mind for worries or desires. As the monks say, true imitation frees the mind for what is essential.

Imitation, as the Shaolin principle teaches us, facilitates deep insights into the essence of others. It reveals their thinking, their feelings and allows us to predict their actions and reactions to our behaviour.

Musashi writes in his *Book of Five Rings* that, 'Becoming the opponent means putting yourself in the opponent's place and thinking from the opponent's point of view. In life there exists a tendency to overestimate the power of the opponent, for example of a robber who locks himself in a house. From the robber's point of view, however, the whole world is against him. The one who is locked in is a pheasant; the one who goes in is a falcon. In individual combat also you must put yourself in your opponent's position.' If you allow yourself to be impressed and believe your opponent has mastered the principles of combat and has a technique superior to yours, you will certainly lose.

People are the worst imitators when they are in a crowd. To demonstrate this, I suggest you conduct a small experiment when you get the chance. The next time you are at a metro, bus or train station, walk so slowly that a crowd forms behind you. Lead this group for a while, then suddenly, make a show of looking at your watch and in the same moment start running. You will be astonished to observe that the group will also suddenly switch pace and start running behind you...

Once I asked an officer in a special police unit, which I had accompanied to a mock hostage drill, how they arrive at their training scenarios. 'We simply try to put ourselves in a criminal's position,' was the answer, 'and think of what we would do in their place.'

In other words, if you want to craft a strategy for getting your way with someone, then you must put yourself in that person's shoes. Let's assume you want to sell me something that I don't want to buy. If you are a weak opponent, you would praise the benefits of the product in superlatives and then be disappointed when I get irritated and end the conversation. You wasted your time and lost a potential customer forever, although this was entirely predictable. Put yourself in my place: if you told me three times you don't want my product and I simply ignore you and continue incessantly with my pitch, how would you react? Exactly.

Anticipate an opponent's arguments

As a strong adversary who fights according to the Shaolin principles, you would have put yourself in my place beforehand. You would have thought in advance about which arguments you yourself would bring up against the product if you did not want to buy it. You would also know what would convince you if you were in my place.

With this kind of preparation, my reaction would not surprise you and you would already have practised your counterarguments. You might still be unable to sell me anything, but you would have learnt a lot about my requirements and would probably have gained a future customer in me.

It is similar when you have a quarrel with someone. When one is in a rage one often uses words to verbally hurt the opponent. These need not be swear words; some people don't use them. In such a situation, carefully observe your opponent's choice of words. If during a really bad fight your opponent calls you 'mean', then this is the word you can use to hit them where it hurts. Even if in your anger you would like to use a retort that goes much further below the belt, don't do it. The opponent is probably immune to such expressions and you would be wasting your energy. For your opponent clearly the worst anyone can be is 'mean'. And that is precisely what your opponent does not want to be.

Win over with empathy

By imitation it is possible not only to predict your opponent's reactions but also to manipulate them. This technique is also known as 'getting on the same wavelength'. People want to feel understood. If during a discussion you contradict someone in their very first sentence, you will have created an opponent who will reject anything that you propose.

However, if you agree with the opponent five times and at the sixth time build on their argument, they will consider you highly competent and be very receptive to your ideas.

The Shaolin principle teaches us that imitation is a very powerful technique. It helps us to understand our opponents, recognise their behaviour and lead them in the direction we want.

EXERCISES

THE CHAMELEON TACTIC

Do you know how imitation can be advantageous for you personally? You will be able to find out with the help of the following questions.

Which animal resembles you the most?

....

Describe the fighting style of a cat.

....

What mistakes have others already made for you?

....

Which of these did you ultimately manage to avoid?

....

Which words do you use when you are angry?

....

What effect exactly do these words have on you?

....

Which habits/kinds of behaviour have you copied from someone else?

....

Why?

....

Those who seize a passing opportunity have no need for pleasant dreams.

Chinese proverb

8. The Principle of Opportunity

By seizing opportunity, the humble and
poor may advance over the noble and rich;
and the small and weak may overcome the big and strong.

Lu Buwei

Learn to create opportunities, wait for them to present themselves, then use them to your advantage and against your opponent.

If you intend to write a book and then publish it, you can approach this goal in two different ways.

The first way starts with a plan. This must be as precise as possible and contain all important points. First, the book itself must be planned: its title, contents, appearance: everything must be noted down. Otherwise what would you have to sell? That is step one.

The next step is to attempt finding a publishing house that wants to publish this very book. The plan also specifies how to go about this: call five publishing houses every day, find out who is in charge and attempt to sell the book concept to them.

Should a publisher want to make changes or publish the book at a later date, the plan specifies moving on and calling the next publishing house. When all thirty publishers on the list have been contacted and there is no positive response, you put the idea to rest. After all, not everyone can write books. That is what the plan says.

The second way follows the principle of opportunity. You decide to write a book and tell all your friends, relatives and acquaintances about it, and wait until the moment is ripe. You know that if it is meant to be, a publisher will approach you to write the book. And if it is not meant to be, then the principle of detachment comes into play, and other interesting opportunities will come along.

Please open your notebook. On an empty page, draw a horizontal line. Under the left end of the line write 'plan' and under the right end write 'opportunity'. Now assess yourself honestly. Are you a person who lives by plans or by opportunities? Make a cross at a point on the line that corresponds with your position. Now reflect on where you would like to be and mark this point with a cross as well. Please repeat this exercise after you have finished reading this chapter.

There is a very large group of people that acts according to plans, and a very small one that acts according to opportunities. Both may have their justifications, yet the 'opportunity group' is usually ahead of the 'plan group'. What the group of planners often tends to overlook is that nothing can be forced, regardless of how good the idea is. 'There is nothing in this world which does not have its decisive moment,' the French statesman Cardinal de Retz once said. Life is not interested in plans and does not go by them. When life considers the time to be right, it offers us an opportunity to fulfil our plans. The winners are those who are ready to seize that opportunity.

'Planners' tend to miss opportunities

People who are fixated on their plan will not even notice the opportunities that blossom to the left and right of the path. They become incapable of registering any other moment and any other path but the one they have decided on.

Seizing an opportunity, however, doesn't just mean going with the flow. The need to plan is a human trait, just as the ability to deviate from the plan when needed—although many people seem to have misplaced the latter ability. Animals will eat when they are hungry and when they find a suitable prey. People tend to eat when it fits in their schedule. If I had to describe planners with one phrase it would be, 'now or never'.

But why should you give up on your dreams simply because life is not the way you expect it to be? If you are not prepared to follow an opportunity, you become an easy opponent. Let us assume that I am your employer and you want a promotion. You plan to come to my office during lunch to inform me that you would like to move to another department. I don't have any objections to your transfer. But what you don't know is that I had to deal with troublesome clients the entire morning. Naturally, you landing up is badly timed. The position you want is in any case not available at the moment and I can't be bothered just then to do anything about it. You achieved nothing and I forget our conversation. When the position does become available later, a colleague I run into at the coffee machine tells me that they are interested. Since I urgently need to fill the position, who do you think will get the job?

The cat and the rat

In Shaolin, a story is told about a farmer who could not get rid of a rat that had got into his house. So he bought a magnificent, strong and brave cat. But in vain. The rat was too quick and outsmarted the cat.

The farmer then got another cat. This one was extremely clever and cunning. But the rat was careful and appeared only when the cat was asleep.

A monk from a nearby temple then loaned him his cat. There was nothing special about this cat. It slept the whole day. The farmer shrugged his shoulders, but the monk insisted on leaving the cat with him. The cat spent all its time sleeping and was indifferent to what was happening around it. Soon, the rat got bolder. It even scurried about in front of the cat, who showed no interest. Until one day, suddenly, the cat pounced and killed the rat with a single blow. This story tells us two things: that it is important to wait for the right moment, and that it is equally important to be ready to act when that moment arrives.

The Shaolin principle teaches us that we can paralyse an opponent for long periods by preventing them from seizing opportunities. We realise how powerful this technique is when we see how often it is applied. Of course, the attacker will camouflage their true intentions. They will sell us their plan and make it appear advantageous for us. Here is an example.

Mobile network provider A has an offer where you get a new mobile phone, apparently free of cost. You understand, of course, that the provider will cover the cost of the phone and consequently sign a twenty-four-month contract at a currently favourable rate. Your hands are tied for the next two years, because even if provider B, C or D were to offer a tariff that is fifty per cent lower two months down the line, you had willingly paid too much and can no longer take advantage of the opportunity.

> Write down three events in your notebook where you were unable to capitalise on an opportunity because either you yourself or your opponent had tied you down.

Anyone acting according to the principle of opportunity will try their level best to act at the right moment, while their opponents will do everything to prevent them from doing so. Opportunities do not arise on their own, even if it may have sounded so. You must sow the seeds at the right time and with a purpose to be able to reap the benefits later on. Of course, you must know along which path the plants will ripen. 'If one does not know to which port one is sailing, no wind is favourable,' the Roman philosopher Seneca said.

Creating opportunities

It might sound like a contradiction but to make optimum use of opportunities we need plans just as much as people who are tied to them. The difference is that this plan describes an objective and not just one way to achieve it.

To return to our earlier example, if you want to write a book then you need such a plan. Simply sitting and waiting for a publisher to call is unlikely to help you achieve your goal. How would anyone know that you want to become a writer? But if you tell many people, all of them will work for you: more people will learn of your desire than you could have possibly managed to personally speak to in ten lives, and probably even some to whom you would otherwise have had no access.

In his famous theory of six degrees of separation, the American psychologist Stanley Milgram proposes that all people on earth are six social connections away from each other. Anyone who lives by the principle of opportunity can benefit from this enormous network. At the same time, creating the opportunity is only half the job done. If we visualise this as fruits growing on a tree, they must be plucked the moment they are ripe and later guarded. You are not the only one eyeing those fruits.

You have surely seen cartoon films where a large number of animals sit gaping at a fruit tree that has just one apple. They all wait with bated breath for the tree to finally drop this one fruit. Whoever gets it will be able to have an excellent meal, which all of them have been looking forward to for a long time. No one pays any attention to the other apple trees in the background that are also dropping fruit. Only one of the animals can get the apple, while the others get nothing. Since they have already spent all their time waiting, they must now take whatever they find if they don't want to starve. Even if an equally delicious apple were to drop from another tree in the near future, they will have to be content with the brown ones on the ground.

The principle of opportunity teaches us to pluck those apples that have just ripened, and to prepare a feast with them. Attempting to force opportunities will only make you go hungry.

Professionally, I frequently meet people who want to set up their own business. They do what everyone advises, namely, they follow a plan: establish a company, find an office, purchase equipment, buy insurance, etc., etc. Once all that is done, they acquire mailing lists and send letters to all potential clients. Then they sit and wait. This is the precise point when the company founder has often already lost.

One could compare this situation to a fighter punching with all their might before the opponent has even appeared. The business costs keep adding up, but there is still no client. No problem, Rome wasn't built in a day. Finally, the first enquiry! 'What, so expensive? I know someone who would do it for half the price!' 'Fine, I need the work, I have a lot of bills to pay, so I'll make you a better offer…'

To anyone who cares to listen, my advice would be to do the exact opposite. Sow the seeds, seize the opportunities that come your way, don't get carried away by grand visions. One swallow doesn't make a summer. Don't waste energy; always calibrate it to the strength of the opponent. You never know who is waiting around the next corner.

Catch the right moment

I once read in a book about the mafia that one of the survival tricks of these gentlemen was to receive guests only when it suited them. We all know that there are suitable and unsuitable moments. Obviously, you can't know which time suits me, but you do know which time suits you.

Personally, I am a night owl. If you wanted a business appointment with me, I would give it only after 11 in the morning, simply because that is the time when I am in the best frame of mind. (Naturally I would not tell you the real reason for the late timing, I would simply say it was because of my staff meeting in the morning.)

If you were my boss and were aware of this, you would schedule all awkward meetings with me as early as possible. We often tend to forget that for everything there is also a time that is right for us personally.

Let us say, you want your boss to sign something without asking too many questions. From reliable sources you learn that on Wednesday they have a lunch appointment with foreign guests where drinks usually flow generously. It would be worth at least considering whether to present the document early on Thursday.

Good warriors will launch their attack when their concentration is at its peak and the adversary's is possibly diverted. As Musashi says, 'In individual martial arts as well, it is essential to be relaxed in body and mind, notice the moment an opponent slackens, and grasp the initiative to win by attacking powerfully and fast.'

When are you in peak form? And when are you most vulnerable? Please write this down in your notebook.

The opportunities to be seized are not restricted just to moments. What set apart the monks of Shaolin from the very beginning was their ability to transform anything into a weapon.

I will never forget how one of them examined my tripod with great interest for its combat worthiness. A shooter without a gun is as helpless as a knight without a sword. It is sufficient to deprive them of their tools to incapacitate them. A really good fighter needs nothing but themselves. Everything else can be found. Be it sand on the ground that can be hurled into the opponent's eyes, a farmer's flail that can be transformed into a deadly weapon or simply a stick with which to keep the opponent at bay.

A Shaolin fighter seizes opportunities that opponents often do not even see. The fighter knows that all the means they need will be available at the place of combat.

Shaolin monks have confidence in their skills and in the principle of opportunity. This is what makes them so unpredictable and dangerous for their opponents.

The principle of opportunity, however, contains yet another powerful technique, namely patience. 'The one who waits patiently at the river will see the corpse of their enemy floating by,' it is said in Shaolin.

The blue and the yellow

There is a tale of the blue people who wage war against the yellow people. Both parties lie hidden in their trenches so that the opponent cannot see them. The yellow people are known for their impatience. The blue people are aware of this and exploit it. After a long silence, blue officer 1 starts shouting, 'Yellow 1, yellow 1!' Promptly comes the reply, 'Yes, here!' And the yellows are another person down. Having lost several of their army in this fashion, the yellows decide to beat the opponents at their own game.

The commander of the yellows shouts loudly, 'Blue 1, blue 1!' No movement. Impatiently, the commander repeats the call. Finally, after the fifth call, a voice from nowhere says, 'Who just called blue 1?' The commander immediately jumps out of the trench and yells, 'Here, it was me…!'

Patience leads to success

In the chapter on imitation you read that the monks in Shaolin mimic drunks. Depending on the situation, they could also act as if they are sleeping or exhausted. The objective remained the same: to lull the opponent, who becomes less cautious, into approaching closer and then attacking them with lightning speed.

Apart from perfect imitation, the path to success lies in true patience. Even when they imitate a sleeping person, fighters must be fully focused on every moment and be ready to strike. If they reveal themselves even a split second too soon, the opponent is warned and the advantage is lost. People sometimes wait for years for the right time to come and then lose everything because they ran out of patience in the final decisive moments. An opponent who can combine opportunity with patience has mastered the element of surprise. Funakoshi Gichin, the founder of modern karate-do, describes it thus, 'When the eagle dives down to attack, it does not spread its wings. Before pouncing on its prey, the tiger makes itself small and flattens its ears. Similarly, the wise allow nothing to betray that they are at the point of springing into action.'

Miyamoto Musashi is said to have been challenged once to a duel by a thirteen-year-old boy, whose father and uncle Musashi had recently defeated. Musashi reached the place of the duel long before the appointed time, found a hiding place and waited. The boy, who was determined to kill him, arrived along with heavily armed followers, but Musashi was nowhere to be seen. It was only when they all believed that he had fled in fear and were about to leave that Musashi stormed out of the shadows and struck down the boy. With both swords Musashi cleaved his way through the crowd and escaped. While the others were still debating what they should do, the samurai had vanished without a trace.

Readiness to act

During the Cold War, when the United States and the Soviet Union were bitter foes, my grandfather attempted to explain to me, what exactly made a dictatorship like the Soviet Union so dangerous. 'If the Americans want to start a war because the moment is strategically favourable, the plan first has to be approved by Congress along with this and that authority. By that time, the opportunity has passed. On the other hand, if the president of the Soviet Union says, in one hour will be a good time for us to strike, then that is what will happen.' While I know today that it isn't quite as simple, I learnt something important. A brilliant method to paralyse an opponent is to engage them as part of a group. As the saying goes, ten people, eleven different opinions, a never-ending debate: 'Could you take on this task, or would it be better for me to do it?'—'We'd have to ask the others, but N is only back on Wednesday…'

The more inflexible an opponent is, the less dangerous they are.

Musashi once said, 'It is easy to gauge the behaviour of a large group of people, because it is difficult to change strategy when you are many, whereas a single person, who acts according to a single decision, is capable of quick changes that are difficult to foresee.'

In a battle, this technique would be used like this: Let's say you and I are colleagues and we have both been waiting a long time for an opportunity that has just emerged. Both of us are prepared, but only one of us will finally make the most of it. In fact, your chances are better than mine, but we need to take our decisions within the next one minute. At the critical moment I ask you, 'Are you absolutely certain that your partner is really fine with this? It would involve quite a change for the two of you…' You can't call your partner to confirm; there isn't enough time. You had already clarified this with them, but at the key moment I manage to weaken and lull you into indecision, and you are out of the running.

Groups may look much more powerful and one therefore

wrongly assumes that there is strength in numbers. But the truly dangerous opponents are those who are lone wolves and agile. An individual can seize passing opportunities, which a group's inertia will prevent it from even considering.

When the monks at the Shaolin temple were called upon for the first time in the year 621 CE to assist in a war against a numerically superior army, the abbot decided to send thirteen monks, an astonishingly low number considering the size of the opposing army. Yet, the dispersed unit of monks was able to win the battle with the help of farmers and their farm tools, which they had repurposed into weapons. To seize opportunities one must be flexible. This must not be confused with ruthlessness or egotism. Take your decisions while you select your target—not when the opportunity has already arisen. It might be too late by then.

Don't lose steam during preparation

Finally, the Shaolin principle teaches us that we must always be a step ahead. In other words, don't be in a position where you start learning only after needing to know something. Then you will always come second.

How many abilities do animals possess that they might never use in their entire lives? Yet should they ever need them, they can summon them up immediately. Why should Shaolin monks strive for extreme perfection if there is no opponent who can match their skill? Because whatever may await, they are equipped. Most people keep chasing lost opportunities all their lives and do not realise it. If someone doesn't get a job only because they don't speak the UgaUga language, they then grit their teeth and decide to learn UgaUga without delay. After all, not knowing the language shouldn't cost them an opportunity the next time. Even though economic ties with the UgaUga country decline with the rise of the AguAgu country, this person goes to the next interview armed with knowledge of the UgaUga language. The job goes to the competitor who speaks a few words of AguAgu.

An Indian proverb says, 'What we have done will not be lost to all eternity. Everything ripens at its time, and becomes fruit at its hour.'

Seize the opportunities that come your way and live your happy dreams.

EXERCISES

HARVESTING APPLES WHEN THEY ARE RIPE

Please answer the following questions to understand how you deal with opportunities. How easy is it to prevent you from seizing opportunities that come your way?

When did you ultimately lose because you lost patience shortly before victory?

....

How can one prevent you from making use of an opportunity, and when was the last time someone did this?

....

Which opportunities would be aligned with what you wish for?

....

Which hoped-for opportunities could you actually seize if they were to present themselves in the next ten minutes?

....

When did you need to chase after an opportunity?

....

Which skill have you acquired just in case you might need it sometime?

....

When was it worthwhile to wait for an opportunity?

....

If you cannot defeat your opponents, you must embrace them.

Chinese proverb

9. The Principle of Yielding

Anger is a wind which blows out the lamp of the mind.

Robert Green Ingersoll

Learn that yielding is simultaneously a form of defence and an attack that the opponent launches against themselves.

The reader might ask: a chapter about yielding in a section on strength? Is the author now backpedalling? Isn't yielding simply a sign of weakness? Am I supposed to run away from my opponents and leave the arena to them without a fight? Certainly not.

In the collection of successful options that we compiled in the last chapter, the ability to yield is the most universal and by far the most powerful. The fact that yielding is considered a weakness also shows us that it belongs in the arsenal of concealed weapons. Opponents can virtually never recognise when we employ it; so it is practically impossible to defend against. Nature shows us that those who can yield will survive.

Lao Tzu once said, 'Stiffness is thus a companion of death, flexibility a companion of life. An army that cannot yield will be defeated. A tree that cannot bend will crack in the wind. The hard and stiff will be broken; the soft and supple will prevail.'

Imagine, for a moment, that nature considered the idea of yielding to be a weakness and therefore did not cater for it. Everything that you bumped into would break in the same instant. Did you just step on a blade of grass? Well, it's crushed now. Your beautiful trees would be destroyed by a light breeze. Why would mice—when they still existed—have run away from cats? Or zebras from lions? Of course, the mouse could prove to itself that it is not a coward and charge into a hopeless fray with the cat. But what would it gain? Most mice prefer life to fame.

Blunting the opponent's force

Some animals have perfected the principle of 'not fighting'. A hedgehog, for example, has no defence technique. When challenged to a fight it reacts with complete refusal. In a best-case scenario, the adversary will expend a lot of energy to no avail and eventually move off.

It works the same way with a human opponent. As we observed with the principle of equanimity, when someone shouts, insults or provokes you in some way, they want to defeat you in a fight. Naturally, your pride does not permit you to ignore the challenge and you accept—with the expected consequences. The Shaolin principle teaches us to yield and thereby allow the opponent's energy to dissipate. Simply don't react, just keep looking at your opponent. At some point, they will feel foolish. Now, if you want to make them really furious and trap them into making a mistake, keep agreeing with them. That is the true art of yielding.

Do not contradict your opponent, instead pour fuel on their fire. Tell them with conviction how right they are, and how stupid you are. Because that is precisely what your opponent does not wish to hear. They will redouble the force of their attack so as to provoke you into defence. What would you gain by that? Let the other person scream and shout until at some point they have used up all their energy and all that they said puts them deep in your debt.

There is, however, one precondition, for the techniques described in this chapter to work.

Your focus must not be on the battle but on the victory; not on demonstrating your bravery but solely on gaining the upper hand.

When we strike a hard object with our fist, the blow is abruptly stopped and a part of the force of impact literally recoils and returns to us. If instead of a wall, however, the target of our blow is a curtain, all our energy is used up in one go.

EXERCISES

THE POWER OF YIELDING

Before we delve deeper into the principle of yielding, I would like to demonstrate to you what it can achieve. Since you need a partner for this exercise, for once you can do this exercise at a time when there is someone with you. Otherwise, please try to do it immediately as usual.

- Stand with your legs firmly on the ground, placed slightly apart. The distance between your feet should be about an arm's length. Tilt your pelvis slightly forward, so that it is aligned above your heels. Close your eyes.
- As described in the chapter on mindfulness, now concentrate on your entire body. Begin with the soles of your feet, feel their connection with the ground. Do you feel how your weight rests on the floor? How you start to root yourself like a tree? Be honest, don't convince yourself, that won't help. It can take five to

ten minutes before this feeling develops. Think about slowness.

- Once you believe you are standing really firmly, call your partner. Their job is to carefully try and imbalance you.
- Your partner will place their hand flat above your chest and push you gently.
- If you now attempt to resist the pressure, you will fall. You are a tree, don't forget. Firmly rooted, and yet capable of yielding.
- Go with the movement, don't resist it. Let your partner slowly increase the force of the push.
- Don't push back, let yourself counterbalance. Do you feel the idea of giving and taking, the principle of yin and yang?

Yin and Yang

Asian philosophy teaches us that these are the two inseparable opposites of life. The dark yin nourishes the light yang; the hard yang protects the soft yin. Yin and yang complement each other and create an indivisible whole. Where there is less of one, there must be more of the other, and vice-versa. While they may be opposites, yin contains yang and is itself contained in it.

It is also said that yang is the principle of change, resulting in action. Its opposite, yin, stands for continuity and produces passiveness and non-action. The action of an aggressive attacker must be countered by passive yielding; the inaction of a passive opponent by the active force of determination.

In combat there are only two ways of applying the technique of yielding. You may dodge to allow the attacking energy of the opponent to pass by. Or you may only pretend to yield to create space for an attack. True yielding, even if it is only for a very short moment, is a very underestimated option for altering the course of a fight.

Boxing match

Do you see the two boxers in a ring? The referee has been inattentive and both of them are in a clinch. Neither wishes to let go for fear the other will take the initiative. Let's say the boxer in red shorts decides to make the first move. The red boxer swings an arm back to pack all his force into a killer punch. If it connects, the fight is over. Does the much smaller boxer in blue shorts stand a chance? Let's watch.

The red boxer sees a chance to win the fight with a technical knock-out and is aware of his physical superiority. Full of confidence, he concentrates all his power into this decisive punch, draws his arm back, strikes… and crashes to the floor with the full force of the blow. Having had no desire to show how well he could roll with the punches, the blue boxer simply stepped back. His goal was not to show which blows he can take but to win the fight. A goal he managed to reach by using the principle of yielding.

Bulldozing doesn't work

It is very similar in everyday life. If you simply sidestep the attack, it flies right past. People who try to bulldoze through everything will only manage to knock themselves out. The principle of opportunity taught us to act at precisely the right moment: not later but also not earlier. A person who cannot yield because their pride is more important to them than their life can be manipulated because they allow themselves to be challenged. They destroy their own chances with their eyes wide open.

'Didn't you say you would do this by March? When are you finally going to do it? You've been saying this for such a long time and putting it off so often, we think you'll never do it because you are too scared…'

A proud, unthinking fighter will fall for this trick. They don't want to be thought of as cowardly so they will act knowing full well that it is too early. On the other hand, someone who follows the principle of yielding will avoid a confrontation. They will say to their challengers, 'Yes, perhaps you are right, and I might never do it. But what is your problem with that? Can someone tell me?' No, naturally no one can, and the matter is closed.

Feigned yielding

The principle of feigned yielding is even more effective because it is almost impossible to spot. Although it is a very common practice, few people are consciously aware of it. The trick is to demonstratively reveal a vulnerability to an opponent, for example, by openly admitting to a crucial weakness. The attacker feels confident and attempts to exploit this seeming advantage, but in doing so they turn the tables on themselves.

Let me give you a practical example. You are having a discussion with me in front of an audience on a topic that you are very conversant with and about which I am fairly clueless—which you suspect. The audience will subsequently vote to decide which one of us is the expert, so you will do everything to make my ignorance obvious.

In the middle of the discussion I will suddenly say, 'There is a seminal sentence on this topic by a famous professor whose name is eluding me just now…' If there is such a sentence and such a person, you will promptly supply the answer and mentally pat yourself on the back.

It would be a mistake on my part to say now, 'Yes, that's exactly who I meant.' Both you and the audience would know that I didn't have a clue and was only saying so not to look stupid. My attack would not only have been futile, but it would also have been turned against me.

In The Art of War, *Sun Tzu writes, 'Pretend to be weak so your opponent may grow arrogant.'*

But if I were to say, 'Of course I know that. No, there is another much more famous person, the name is at the tip of my tongue…,' then I would have won. Naturally, there is neither a second person nor a second sentence, but you and the audience don't know that. Both of you now consider me the expert since you hadn't even heard of this famous professor. More importantly, I would have shaken your confidence. Thoughts like, 'What does this joker know that I don't?' or 'Whom could he mean?' would weaken you. An important technique of feigned yielding is that of 'apparent inferiority'.

Allowing a tactical 'victory'

People are so greedy to win over others that when they see an opportunity to do so they forget everything else. This is what happens at auctions. I have heard of people who bought used objects they had no need for at prices that far exceeded those of a brand-new product. Just because they couldn't back down.

But it can go even further. 'How about a three per cent discount? That's too low for you? I can't give you more than five per cent. You're saying you would buy it if I gave you ten per cent? I can't afford to lose a customer like you.

Very well. Would you like me to pack it?' The fact that even with a twenty per cent discount from me you would still have paid me more than what you would have paid at the shop next door without any discount simply escaped you in the heat of the moment. Yet the apparent victory was yours.

But my victory was real because I would never have sold the product at the original price anyway—your discount was already factored in.

I once heard of a candy store in America that was bought over by a large supermarket chain. Although the new owners did not change the prices, there was suddenly a sharp drop in their main customers—children. When the children were asked about it, they said they used to get more candies for their money in the old shop. In fact, the owner of the candy store would always put a little less in the bag before weighing it and then add some more. The salesperson in the supermarket did the exact opposite and would then take out the extra candy from the bag. Graphic designers often include small mistakes in their design jobs. These are so obvious that the client immediately spots them. It gives the customer the feeling that they are one up on the professionals.

The Shaolin principle teaches us always to give our opponents room for an apparent victory. Or as Sun Tzu says:

'When you surround an army, leave an outlet free. Do not press a desperate foe too hard. This does not mean allowing the enemy to flee. It is to allow the enemy to believe there is a way to safety, for if a foe is cornered, they must fight for their lives and will do so with the strength of desperation.'

Many people are blinded by their own pride about the true intentions of their opponents. Keichu, a great Zen teacher, was the head of a cathedral in Kyoto. One day, the governor of Kyoto came to see him for the first time. Keichu's attendant handed him the visiting card of the governor on which was written, 'Kitagaki, Governor of Kyoto'. 'I will have nothing to do with such a fellow,' Keichu told the attendant. 'He has no business here. Tell him to get out.' The attendant handed the card back with an excuse. 'That was my mistake,' the governor said and with a pencil crossed out the words, 'Governor of Kyoto'. 'Ask your master again.' 'Oh, is that Kitagaki?' exclaimed the master when he saw the card. 'I would like to see him.'

I recall my grandmother telling me the difference between the arrogant, less successful people of country A and the highly successful but more down-to-earth people of country B.

'In country A,' she explained, 'if a spot on the floor has to be cleaned, the boss calls their secretary, who informs the assistant to bring in the cleaning staff. Four persons are tied up with this one task.'

'On the other hand, in country B, for the same spot, the boss changes from their jacket into a white overall, wipes the spot, wears the jacket again and is back to being the boss.'

The crane and the snake

Novices at the Shaolin monastery do not start with martial arts training right away.

They must first consciously learn to do lowly tasks so that they shed their pride. The principle of yielding plays an important role even in the Shaolin martial arts techniques. There is a story about a monk who observed a crane fighting a snake. The bird made rapid, repeated jabs at the snake, without however managing to hit it. The snake didn't snap back, didn't make any threatening moves, but dodged the attacks with slow, fluid movements. Finally the crane gave up exhausted and went off. The monk saw in this fight an affirmation of the old idea that the soft defeats the hard, that yielding is victorious against attack. From this principle of opposites, of yin and yang, he developed a martial arts form that later became famously known as tai chi.

Allow opponents to defeat themselves

Imagine the following situation: the department manager in your company is known to be an aggressive person and colleagues fear him. He starts shouting at the slightest pretext and constantly tries to run down his subordinates. However, since the performance of the department meets management targets, the view about him is that he is a pleasant colleague and a good boss. Nevertheless, the company management promises that it will take action if there is a concrete case.

The next time this boss starts screaming and shouting about something that is entirely unjustified, you can react in two ways. Either you can yell back and tell the boss what an idiot he is. You might even be right, but this could end badly for you. After all, you shouted at your boss and you were both equally aggressive. The better course of action would be to stay calm, even if it is difficult at that moment. It will draw attention to the fact that your boss is shouting at someone who is quiet and composed, and your boss's boss who might be passing by will see this or the incident will be conveyed to them by a colleague.

The Shaolin principle teaches us that the soft triumphs over the hard. Yielding is a form of defence, but at the same time it is an attack that the opponent launches against themselves.

Game of chess

When young monks in Shaolin are learning how to mentally prepare themselves for the technique of imitation, they are told the story of a young man who went to a Zen monastery. He explained to the master, 'I am seeking nirvana but I do not have the endurance to persist with anything for any length of time. I could never bear to do years of meditation and follow strict discipline. Is there a path to enlightenment even for someone like me?'

'There is a way,' the master replied. 'What have you concentrated on the most in your life till now?'

The young man pondered. 'Actually, the only thing that I was ever really interested in is chess. I spent most of my time on that.'

'Very well,' said the master and asked for an old, experienced monk to be called who was a good chess player. The monk arrived with a chess set under his arm and the master asked him to set up the pieces.

Then the master pulled out his sword and said with all his authority, 'You will now play a game of chess. The loser will have his head struck off.'

Both men sensed that the master was serious and began their game. The young man noticed how beads of sweat formed on his forehead and how the chess board before him became his entire world. He was completely focused on every move. Initially, things were not going his way, but then his opponent made a hasty move and he was able to systematically start destroying the monk's defence.

As he captured the monk's pieces one by one, he furtively glanced at the monk's face. It was an honest face, exalted by years of meditation and seeking enlightenment. He thought of his own worthless life and a wave of compassion washed over him. He deliberately made a mistake, then another.

Suddenly, the master bent over and pushed the board and pieces to the ground. Facing the boy, he said, 'There is never a winner or a loser. Two things are important for the path to enlightenment: concentration and compassion. Today you have learnt both. Your concentration was complete and yet you felt compassion. Stay here and train your soul in this attitude, and you will achieve nirvana.'

EXERCISES

THE SOFT DEFEATS THE HARD

Deep down most people believe that they are very soft. The questions below will show you where you really stand.

In which situations do you find it difficult to give in?

....

Why?

....

Would you do business with a person who flatly refused to address you by your title?

....

When did you get fooled by an 'apparent yielding'?

....

When have you won by giving in?

....

Do you always need to have the last word?

....

Find an example in which the soft wins over the hard.

....

How would your counterpart react if they were angry?

....

Part Three

Learn to Win

A wise man achieves victory by doing only what needs to be done without using violence.

Lao Tzu

Supreme excellence consists in breaking the enemy's resistance without fighting.

Sun Tzu

10. The Principle of Superiority

Draw the bow, but don't shoot—it is better to be feared than to be hit.

Chinese proverb

Learn that true superiority is the art of winning without fighting.

A story is told in Shaolin about a king who wished to have a very strong gamecock. He therefore ordered a monk to train the gamecock. The monk began by teaching the gamecock the technique of fighting.

After ten days the king asked, 'Can I now organise a fight for the cock?' But the trainer replied, 'No, no! He is strong, but it is hollow strength. All he wants to do is fight.

He is excited and his strength is erratic.'

Ten days later the king asked again, 'Can the contests begin now?'—'No, no, not yet!' was the reply. 'He is still very hot-headed. All he wants is to fight. When he hears another cock, even if it is in the neighbouring village, he is instantly enraged and wants to rush headlong into a skirmish.'

After another ten days the king again asked, 'What about now?' This time the trainer replied, 'He is now able to control his emotions, and when he hears or sees another cock, he remains calm. His bearing is erect and displays a powerful tautness. He no longer flies into a rage, and his strength and energy are not just superficial.' During the tournament, no other bird was capable of even challenging the king's gamecock, they all fled in fear. He didn't need to fight. He had gone beyond the stage of technicalities and was superior to them all.

Being superior begins in the mind

One must know that being superior is not a character trait but a principle. Power is not something one receives like a reward. It is something that one seizes; it is something that resides in the mind.

Let me give you an example. Let's assume you and I both own a villa. We are both very rich, both houses are lavish, appear equally valuable and are thus equally attractive for criminals. The one thing that might influence burglars in selecting their target could be a stubborn rumour.

In the village there is talk of a very aggressive and vicious guard dog in my house, who has already torn another thief to pieces. Which house do you think will be broken into next? I don't possess a guard dog and the dog hasn't killed anyone. But the rumour that I've circulated is sufficient. I have demonstrated my superiority over the burglars. In all probability they will pay a visit to your villa.

EXERCISES

NOBODY IS INVINCIBLE

When you read the title of this chapter you probably asked yourself: can superiority be a principle? How can I be superior to someone who ranks above me? Before we look into this question, please take out your notebook.

- Place the notebook horizontally and divide a double page into three columns.
- In the left column write the names of three persons who you think are superior to you.
- In the second column write down what characterises these persons. Are they particularly strong, rich, do they have many titles or are they very unscrupulous? Please find five traits for each person.

- In the third column, finally, write how to defeat these persons. E.g., someone who can hit very hard can be defeated by the principle of yielding; a rich person through their greed.

Think about this thoroughly. Nobody is invincible. Which of these so-called traits have you actually put to the test?

A few years ago, I visited an orphanage with two Shaolin monks. The monks showed their best moves, and the youngsters followed the performance, mouths agape in admiration. During the ensuing discussion, one of them wanted to know what it meant to fight so well that one didn't need to fight.

I replied, 'Neither of these two monks touched you. But would you challenge them to a fight?' You might be asking yourself now, if it is really that simple, why don't more people seize power?

Subservience is a comfort zone

Because many simply do not want to. Looking up to others has many seeming advantages. One needn't think for oneself, one carries out instructions that others give, there is no responsibility; after all, someone else took the decisions. One has peace and doesn't have to constantly fight.

But like so many other things, the principle of fighting is a natural impulse that is embedded deep within us. From a moral perspective, fighting is neither good nor bad. Nature does not think in these categories. If an unwanted guest enters an animal's territory, it will attack without hesitation. That is why we respect animals and usually do not enter their domain. The same goes for people who are said to have power and strength. Many look up to them unthinkingly and allow themselves to be put under pressure by such people. Do you want an example?

By post you receive a letter that says, 'If you do not pay me the amount of 20 euros soon, I will file a complaint in court and you will have to pay with interest.' You toss the letter in the dustbin thinking, 'Sure, go ahead. I don't think a court will entertain a case for 20 euros.' You don't pay this ridiculous amount because you know that the demand is unjustified.

Don't fear paper tigers

Same situation, a different letter: 'On behalf of my client I am sending you a final demand notice to transfer without delay to our account the outstanding amount of EUR 20.07 along with reminder and processing fees amounting to a total of EUR 57.62, failing which we shall be obliged to recover the amount without further notice by way of legal proceedings.'

Would you still not pay? You would probably think, why quarrel with a lawyer. If they really go to court who knows what connections they might have. But you don't owe this amount! You already learned in the chapter on mindfulness that the writer of this letter could be just some random person. And by now you must have understood that for many people, this method of putting others under pressure is a good way of making money. We only need to decide to do something.

When I had just started off on my own professionally and had to invoice my first assignments, it was a big drama every time. First, the opportune moment had to be found: Dear client, can we now settle accounts? Is the assignment actually complete? Might the client want some changes before I can bill them? I would examine each and every item on the invoice—was it justified, not too expensive?

I did this until I finally began to learn from those who were clearly superior to me. 'Three minutes advice over the phone? No problem. The bill is in the post. Too expensive? No worries, there's no compulsion to call me.'

If you want to gain the upper hand, you must be prepared to fight. You must stop believing that opponents will do what is morally right and accept that often this is not the case. And you must learn to fight well so that at some point you no longer need to fight at all.

Superiority does not need affirmation

In the last chapter you learnt a lot about human behaviour. One trait that kept coming up and which also makes you extremely vulnerable is pride.

Let's recall: if I were to tell you that I'm so pleased you are one of the few people who really understands my book, it would probably make you feel proud. Making you feel proud would make me happy, and by itself there is nothing wrong with that. However, if in the future you prefer my books to those of other authors who did not say this to you, I have managed to manipulate you. The Shaolin principle teaches us to feel good from the innermost depths of our being.

For example, you might, for whatever reason, think it's great to colour your hair in green and blue stripes. Socially, you can afford to do so. You love your new hairstyle, but people on the street give you funny looks. Acquaintances make snide remarks. Your inner struggle begins. Thoughts like, 'I guess their reaction is understandable. It's not really the done thing, is it? Maybe it's okay when one is on holiday, but not here.' Might I intervene here and ask why you are bothered about what other people think?

If you are dependent on external praise, you become vulnerable to attack. You will always be subservient to those whom you want to please at any cost.

You like your hair as it is, and yet, because you feel it is more important to meet other people's expectations than your own, you colour your hair back to its original colour. This is the precise moment at which you lose the fight. Others have been successful in demonstrating their power over you.

What does this have to do with power? Let's be honest: what possible reason is there to get irritated by someone else's hairstyle? None, really. But there are people who are bothered when others try to break free of the straitjacket imposed by society. 'I'd like to do that myself but I don't dare, so no one else should do it either.' Now, if the 'rebels' seem diffident and on the back foot, it arouses the fighting instinct in others. In fact, the hairstyle itself does not concern the attackers. If a pop star were to colour their hair in the exact same style a week later, they would applaud their genius and admire the unique hairdo. 'Of course they can do it, that's a pop star's prerogative! No question of attacking them about it—pop stars are way above us.'

Write down in your notebook what distinguishes you from this pop star. To avoid any misunderstanding, please note that if you provoke simply to be provocative then you have misunderstood something. Please read the preceding chapters again.

Being superior means winning the fight before even entering the battlefield. You have seen how people gain power over us because they seize it, and we give it to them.

'Not the wind, but the sail determines the direction,' says a Chinese proverb. Symbols of power are an interesting way to explain this idea. Some animals play dead when a powerful opponent approaches. They offer no defence to the impending danger, hoping that it will pass them by. If you want to catch such animals, you only need to threaten them in a way that they recognise.

It's the same with people. They allow themselves to be blinded by the opponent's mask and in the bargain completely forget to take any action. A person in a suit or in uniform appears to be a figure of authority to us, and that paralyses our thinking and our defences. We are so afraid of the supposed power of such persons that we carry out their instructions unquestioningly. What I don't understand is that such suits and uniforms can be bought in any shop. They reveal absolutely nothing about the person wearing them. Do you still remember the train conductor?

On my travels through Asia, I often travelled by night train. Once I was rudely woken up in the middle of the night by two armed, uniformed persons, who stood before me threateningly and wanted me to pay for something that I didn't understand. It had something to do with a seat reservation. I refused to pay and both of them became increasingly aggressive, demanding the money. It was only when I took out a pen and paper and began to make a show of noting down their IDs that they did an immediate about turn. One of them mumbled it must have been a misunderstanding, everything was alright. And then they were gone.

Symbols of power merely set the stage

We should never allow ourselves to be blinded by symbols of power, and we ourselves must act decisively. Official identity cards are a notch above uniforms for brandishing power.

These are important-looking pieces of paper with a photo and innumerable stamps and seals. The paper contains information about who the person showing the card apparently is and what they are consequently allowed to do. Often, an identity card can give the holder unfettered power. Everyone loves identity cards, whether they are service passes, press cards, etc. My laser printer can print them all.

Lacking a press pass in Asia once, I modified my blood donor card into one: paste a passport photograph, sign and it's ready. How would a clerk in Asia know what my identity card should look like? Of course, an identity card alone is not enough; the mannerisms also have to match. If I were to timidly ring your doorbell, wait apprehensively on the landing until you finally opened the door, diffidently introduce myself as an employee of XY government agency who has come to search your apartment, you would likely have doubts about my identity. With a bit of bad luck you might even find out that the agency doesn't exist. On the other hand, it would be quite different if I knocked loudly on your door and entered your apartment quicker than you could open your mouth, flashing my ID in passing. Naturally, you wouldn't check it. It might be real! Yes, so? Do you not have the right to know who comes into your apartment?

One does not receive power, one seizes it.

I witnessed this principle practised to perfection when I was once in Nepal. A group that had just climbed a very high peak arrived at the airport. In Nepal one needs a special permit for climbing, which is issued on a piece of paper.

Before the group could pass customs, they were intercepted by a man in an elaborate uniform who collected these permits from them. The group pleaded and begged to be allowed to keep them as souvenirs. A short while later, the mountain climbers—minus 20 dollars each but with their permits—passed through customs. The moral of the story? Of course one was not obliged to give up these permits. But almost anyone can be defeated by audacity. One noteworthy feature of superiority is that it requires the presence of its inverse—someone who is subordinate. That does not mean that we should start subordinating others. This would contradict the Shaolin principle. But we should be aware that those whom we regard as superiors are doing precisely that. And we allow them to do so with our eyes wide open.

> Please take out your notebook. Now, imagine yourself in the following situation. Someone you regard as your superior has done you an obvious injustice. However, you believe you cannot defend yourself against this person and therefore think you are not in a position to rectify the situation. What exactly are you afraid of? Please note this down. Then write next to it what this person could actually do to you.

Fear of the 'boss'

When we are told to report to the boss because the boss apparently is unhappy with our work, we usually get a sinking feeling in the pit of our stomach, even if we know that we did our work properly.

This gives your opponent power and, without your wanting, it also puts them at a huge advantage. The principle of superiority teaches us to assess the true strength of an adversary and to react precisely to this. What could the boss actually do? Even if they wanted to cut your pay or sack you, if your work has been in order you can discount this possibility simply on legal grounds. Your boss will also not beat you or shout at you. At the very worst, your boss may say that in their personal opinion your work is terrible. You could live with that, couldn't you?

Your boss, who was expecting you to be cowed down, will be quite irritated that they are no longer in a position of superiority and what they are saying to you does not affect you in any way.

Musashi writes, 'Under the sword lifted high, there is hell making you tremble. But go ahead without hesitation, a land of bliss awaits you.'

Until a short while ago, there used to be customs officers at border crossings who obviously enjoyed harassing hapless travellers. Of course, I know that they are only doing their job, but one can also go too far.

Once I arrived at a border post where an obviously bored officer awaited me. Sullenly he indicated to me to get out and open the boot of my car. It was instantly clear to me that this was a power game, and I also knew that any resistance or any obvious sign that I was in a hurry would backfire. It wasn't unusual for people to spend five hours at such border crossings. With exaggerated cheerfulness I got out of the car, opened the boot and immediately also opened a suitcase and asked the officer what else I could show him. He was so taken aback by my reaction that he made no further demands. Three minutes later the potential nightmare was over.

The Shaolin principle teaches us to make superiority a principle. Even a supposedly weak fighter can defeat a seemingly stronger opponent if they confront them without fear.

EXERCISES

BECOME MORE SELF-ASSURED

Using the questions below, assess your attitude to power and superiority. What could you improve?

What does superiority mean to you?

....

What does power mean?

....

Who do you think you are superior to?

....

Why?

....

What would this person need to change to become superior to you?

....

When did someone defeat you simply by seizing power?

....

When have you been defeated by sheer audacity?

....

The monkey and the crane

In Shaolin, a story is told of an aged master who one day observed a big monkey attacking a crane. The bird showed no fear whatsoever and landed a powerful blow on its opponent with one of its wings. Then it hopped on its other leg, hit out again with its wing and at the same time swiftly gouged one of the monkey's eyes. Screaming with pain, the monkey ran into the forest. The crane preened its feathers and flew off into the sky.

The idea of superiority is regarded highly by the monks. If a master is defeated by a student in a fight, the master's prestige remains intact but they can no longer consider themselves to be the student's teacher. The monks must therefore continue to remain fit well into old age.

The patriarch Lin Wo was famous for taking on thirty trained fighters in succession without being hit a single time. At the same time, as the Shaolin principle teaches us, true superiority is in the mind.

Lao Tzu said that the greatest teachers are those whose students surpass them: 'When the student is ready, the teacher will appear. When the student is truly ready, the teacher will disappear.'

There doesn't even need to be a fight because someone who is truly superior need not fight to win.

Immutable—then your heart
remains bound for eternity.

Ryokan

11. The Principle of Letting Go

By letting go, everything happens by itself.
The world is mastered by those who let go.

Lao Tzu

Learn to let go of the opinions adopted from others and constantly review your own.

When Alexander the Great faced the challenge of undoing an intricate knot connecting a cart's yoke and shaft, an unusual approach had to be found. Many clever and strong men before him had already tried and failed. Alexander detached himself from all previous methods and simply cut through the knot with his sword.

Think of the following situation: three pistol shooters—

one poor, one average and one a crack shot—engage in a three-way duel. The poor shooter hits the target once in ten shots, the average shooter hits it in half the time and the ace shooter never misses.

The duel is to take place in two rounds, with the shooters taking turns at shooting. It is agreed that the worst shooter will shoot first, then the average and finally the excellent one, and the second round will continue in the same sequence. What should the worst shooter now do?

> If you think you have found a solution, take a step back and try to find an even better one. Please write your idea in your notebook.

If the poor shooter wants to survive, their best option is to shoot in the air. The average shooter, whose turn is next, will most certainly aim at the excellent shooter, fearing that the excellent shooter will target them next. If the average shooter hits, it is the poor shooter's turn again. If the average shooter misses, the crack shot will first fire at the average shooter because they feel superior to the poor shooter—who after all succeeds only once in ten shots.

The eleventh Shaolin principle teaches us to approach each situation afresh. It teaches us that we must constantly let go of everything that we believe we know: seemingly tried and tested methods or preconceived solutions.

In either case, the poor shooter will have one opponent less and will certainly survive the first round.

On the other hand, had the poor shooter aimed at the crack shooter, as you might have assumed, and perhaps even hit, how would the situation have ended?

The carpenter and the emperor

Another story told in Shaolin is of a master carpenter who was commissioned by the emperor to build a cupboard for the palace bedroom. The carpenter, a Zen monk, told the emperor that he would not be in a position to work for five days. The emperor's spies observed that the monk sat around the entire time, apparently doing nothing. Then, once the five days were over, the monk got up. Within three days he had fashioned the most extraordinary cupboard anyone had ever seen. The emperor was both extremely satisfied and intrigued. He bade the monk to come to him and asked what he had done in the five days before he started his work. The monk replied:

'I spent the entire first day letting go of all thoughts about failure, fear and being punished if my work did not please the emperor.

'The entire second day I spent letting go of all thoughts about not being capable, about not possessing the skills to make a cupboard worthy of the emperor.

'The entire third day I spent letting go of all hopes and desires for fame, glory and reward if I were to make a cupboard that met with the emperor's approval.

'The entire fourth day I spent in letting go of the pride that could take root in me if I were successful in my task and I were to receive praise from the emperor.

'And the entire fifth day I spent contemplating in my mind a clear vision of this cupboard in the certainty that even an emperor would wish for it in the form it is before you now.'

Recognise your biases

Were one to ask any random person if they had biases, one would usually get an immediate 'no' in response. After all, everybody is unbiased and objective! Really? Let's say I show you a photograph that is dark and obviously out of focus. I tell you that the picture was taken by an elderly gentleman going on eighty. Do I see you nodding knowingly? For such an old person, in fact, the picture is not bad. Of course, the photo has technical flaws, but one should look beyond those in this case. But it's not a great picture.

If I were now to reveal to you that this person is one of the world's most famous photographers, be honest, would you still regard the picture in the same way? Or would you suddenly realise that the underexposure and blurred effect are brilliant design elements? After all, such a famous photographer would surely know what they are doing!

> You are evaluating an exactly same photograph differently. Why? Bias perhaps? Write down the answer in your notebook.

In his book, *Into Thin Air*, in which he provides an eyewitness account of the drama on Mt Everest in 1996, Jon Krakauer describes that not being able to let go of one's biases can even end lives. Descending from the summit, he encountered a guide who had accompanied the group. Although the man was behaving oddly, it did not occur to Krakauer that the man might be having problems. 'Had I met him under different circumstances,' he would later write, 'it would have been instantly clear to me that he was oxygen deprived. But at that point he was just our experienced guide, someone we naturally looked up to. I couldn't dream that someone like that could be experiencing a problem.' Unfortunately, this wrong assumption cost Andy Harris his life.

Biases are weapons in the hands of an opponent

For an opponent, preconceived opinions are a godsend. They function as a hook to catch the adversary and push them where one would like to have them.

The great thing about this from our opponent's perspective is that no one ever checks their biases. Imagine that you are about to buy a lovely jacket at a fantastic discount. It so happens that I also want to buy this jacket. I am aware of how opposed you are to people belonging to a certain group 'X'. You already have the jacket in your hand and are about to pay when I say, 'Oh, that looks like it's been made by one of those X people. Isn't this their typical design?' That should suffice for me to be the one buying the jacket.

Even though an X person certainly did not design the jacket, let alone manufacture it, your dislike for this group is so strong that you only see what you are made to see.

This is how it works with everything. It's good if it comes from group A, bad if it's from group B. How else to explain that for many people it makes a difference if someone from their country is involved in a terrible accident where there are over 300 casualties. It's only half as bad if the victims are from country Z.

If you did not know them personally, what is the difference between a dead Indian, American or Austrian and a dead Nigerian? Please write this down in your notebook.

In fact, we all have many biases that lead us to make subconscious judgements. It starts with us visualising how someone looks based on their name. As long as we have only heard of a person and not met them, we will always associate this face with them. We like them or reject them without really knowing anything about them simply on the basis of their name.

Let's take the name Peter. If someone had a step uncle by that name whom they hated, they will not be able to dissociate from negative emotions when they meet a person by that name. On the other hand, if Peter was the name of the family's best friend, this same person would be guaranteed a warm reception.

Remember, it need not be people with whom one associates emotions. As someone with no mountaineering experience, would you accompany me to the 'Devil's Paw'? I doubt it. It already sounds very high and dangerous! The same applies to colours, smells, places or music that arouse certain emotions in you and cloud your judgement.

Whenever you come across something like this in the future, mentally turn it around. Imagine the good as bad and the bad as good.

> Find five terms or names that you associate with good or bad things. Note these down and also why you feel that way. Now try and imagine the same term with opposite features. I don't mean that you should imagine the good Peter to be bad, but try and imagine any Peter with negative qualities. How would someone like that look?

If a name is associated so strongly with a particular person that you find it impossible to like someone solely because they have the same name, simply give them a pet name.

If you think that you will not like a particular dish because it contains this or that, just forget you know. Taste it as if you had no idea about the ingredients. And do this afresh each time.

Conditioned at an early age

The first time that most people are confronted with preconceived notions is in their childhood. Many children are conditioned to accept that everything adults say is right. This gets so ingrained that even when they grow up, they are unable to critically examine these opinions. This is how rigid behavioural patterns develop.

In your notebook please write down five opinions, prejudices or supposed facts that you adopted from your parents, teachers or other caregivers without ever verifying them. Please also write alongside why you are so certain that these are right. Perhaps you can review your answers during a quiet moment.

When people are born, they have no idea of the society they will be a part of for their entire lives. They know nothing about its morals, its values or its judgements. They do not know what is considered good or bad, or what is desirable and undesirable. They are not aware of what is allowed and what is forbidden. If such people are allowed to do as they wish, they would of course be free, but they would be completely unpredictable for everyone else. They would do things because they considered them necessary, not because they thought these were desired.

Every 'new' person is therefore allotted a place in society. Like new employees, they are familiarised with the company's vision and mission. As long as the new entrant has not been formally inducted, they can be assigned to any department.

If you were born into a criminal family, you would almost certainly have a different view of killing than the child of a priest's family. As the former, you would, of course, also more realistically assess your own chances of being killed by someone. Just because you yourself would not do something does not mean that someone else may not do it. Apart from the moral compass, certain associations are also formed that last a lifetime.

It is interesting that such linkages do not depend primarily on personal experiences but on adopted opinions.

Police personnel, I am sure you will agree, are upright people. After all, they are representatives of the state and guarantee law and order. So, even though you do not personally know any police officer, you will always approach them with a certain respect. (But if your family was involved in organised crime, how would you approach the same officer? You still don't know them.)

'Demand much from yourself, little from others, and you will prevent discontent,' said Confucius.

If you were to observe a police officer or someone in police uniform attack someone else on the street, you probably wouldn't think much and just assume that the person in uniform was right. Why should a policeman attack anyone? Well, why not? It is absolutely plausible that someone whose principle in life is to help others would choose to join the police. But unfortunately, the reverse is not a valid statement, namely that all who join the police follow this principle in life.

The principle of being able to let go teaches us that an opponent may attack even in places, which in our opinion they cannot or should not. In a battle, anyone who is not able to let go of preconceived opinions is like a statue that can look in only one direction. As children we used to play a game called knock and run. Actually it was more of a dare to show how brave you were. The dare consisted in ringing one or several doorbells and then running away as quickly as possible. Being caught by angry residents could have unpleasant consequences. The opponent then was very clear: three children scurrying off. Who else would it have been?

Today the situation would be quite different. The mischief-makers wouldn't be caught. They are, of course thirty years older. It's not because they can run much faster but because nobody would suspect them. As an adult, one can simply ring a bell and calmly walk away. A window opens on the first floor. 'Did you see that? These bratty XY kids! Ring the bell and just run off!' Naturally it was the children. Why would an adult do something like that?

Well, why not? Because the adult hopefully received an upbringing that the children still lack? Or because they themselves learnt as children that adults are infallible and only do what is right and good?

Expect the unexpected

Imagine you are a narcotics officer. When a young man with long, unwashed hair, torn jeans, stinking of smoke and alcohol, walks past you on the street, and behind him is a businessman in a custom-tailored suit, perfect haircut, shiny shoes, and smelling of expensive aftershave, whom would you search?

I'm afraid it would probably be the young man. Tough luck for you if they were both working together and wanted to provoke that reaction because the businessman was carrying the drugs. Now you should be the one asking yourself, 'why not?' In the examples mentioned above, the opponent was stronger because they employed the weapon of letting go and were confident that it was a weapon you did not possess.

The fact that we take so many ideas we grew up with to be the gospel truth without reflecting on them is also illustrated in the notion of 'big boys/girls don't cry'.

A grown-up is brave, strong and doesn't show emotions. Many of us learn even as children to bottle up our feelings. We think this is natural, and later on even consider it right. 'You can't cry in front of everyone! Come on, here's a hanky. There, there, it's fine now.'

Perhaps we should reverse this for a change: give our sadness free rein and completely hide our joy. If something happens for which we have been waiting for years or if we are given a wonderful gift, we receive it without displaying any emotion.

A never-ending story

The insidious thing about the principle of upbringing is that our opponents can rely on it always being passed on unchanged.

Even when there are things that clearly create obstacles in our lives, which we think are just plain wrong, we still pass them on unchanged to the next generation. Not because we find them great but because we simply cannot let go of the thought that those who passed them on to us could never be wrong. And those things never harmed us, right? Another fallacious conditioning is that certain people or institutions must be trusted. Of course, they might mean well, perhaps their actions are also benign, but does that mean that they must always be so?

> Please write five things in your notebook that you have recognised to be wrong and do not want to pass on to the next generation.

In Japan this conditioning goes so far that it is considered extremely impolite to check the change one receives. Once again, it is necessary to be able to let go. As Lenin said, 'Trust is good, control is better.'

Try and treat all opponents equally: not with any particular mistrust, but also not with unfounded trust. A service provider who inserts many footnotes in extra small print in their price chart, which conceal the conditions about the conditions, definitely wants to avoid giving you information about the true cost.

If the service provider's intentions were honest, they could simply write: 'Our services cost so and so much.' Even if you get something for 'free' or as a 'gift' you know that you have obviously paid for it somewhere.

> Why should anyone give you a gift? Please note down why you would prefer a seller who apparently gives you a gift.

Someone who is unconsciously attached to things is easily manipulated by an opponent. It's an interesting fact that your objectivity towards an attacker reduces in direct proportion to how personally close you are to that person. Everyone knows that in politics or in large corporations, things are not always above board. Now and again, there is misappropriation of funds by governments or companies. But individual officers or employees would never do that. So then who did?

Positive bias also clouds judgement

For many people, demonstrating trust seems to be some sort of a duty. Let's suppose I want a service from you but don't want to pay for it. You smell a rat and ask me for advance payment. My affronted, 'What, you don't trust me?' will suffice, and you will hastily withdraw the demand for advance payment. But why should you feel obliged to trust me?

One of the most important ideas that a good fighter must know how to let go of is the urge to judge everything. There are cheap things and expensive ones; important and unimportant things; good and bad. Seemingly good persons could have bad sides, and seemingly bad persons could have good points. Do you remember the principle of yin and yang?

I remember well a friend from my childhood. He would casually carry his expensive camera in his hand, without the strap. I myself could never do that, I was too scared I would drop such a valuable item. When I told him about my concern, he gave me some very convincing advice: 'Imagine that you are carrying a stone instead of a camera. A stone doesn't just drop from your hand, does it? Just forget how expensive the thing is and you'll also forget your fear of letting it fall!'

An important quality of a good fighter is to understand that people always act for a reason. Not a good reason and not a bad reason, but a reason.

Shaolin kung fu has been perfected to such an extent over the last 1500 years that even the position of the little finger is significant. The opponent does not retreat because they are cowardly and afraid—even though you might wish that—but because it is part of their technique. Every step, every movement, however small, has a reason and a purpose.

A shopkeeper who sells you something at a discount or even gives you a gift, does not do this to make you happy. Take a step back and detach yourself from this notion, even though it may seem difficult at first. You will be surprised to recognise the true intentions behind such actions.

Being able to let go also means achieving the ability to focus on what is essential. 'The wisdom of life consists in eliminating what is unessential,' according to a Chinese saying. In any case, these are primarily things that we cannot change.

Lao Tzu said, 'By letting go, everything happens by itself. The world is mastered by those who let go.' The Shaolin principle teaches us that we must truly live this letting go.

EXERCISES

RIDDING YOURSELF OF BIASES

Even though most of us don't think so, in fact, we all have biases that weaken us at decisive moments. The questions below should help you to identify these and to let go of them.

Which opinions that you acquired in childhood do you want to let go of?

....

What would you have done differently from the way your parents brought you up?

....

In an emergency, whom would you trust more: a judge or a drug dealer?

....

Why?

....

Where do you need to learn to let go?

....

The mind is everything.
You are what you think.

The Buddha

12. The Principle of Self-Knowledge

If you want to defeat others, you must first defeat yourself;
if you want to lead others, you must first lead yourself;
if you want to know others,
you must first know yourself.

Lü Buwei

Learn, that everything you are and will become lies only within you.

'Everyone sees what you appear to be, few experience what you really are,' wrote the great Italian statesman Niccolò Machiavelli.

Most people have quite a precise idea of how others should view them: as big, strong, talented, generous, just, good-looking, articulate and universally loved. Regardless of what they are really like, they do everything to live up to this image.

It's rare, however, for the external appearance to match the essence of the person behind it. Everyone wants to be something, just not what they really are. Add to that the expectations of people around us. They too have an idea of what we should be like. Whatever corresponds to this idea is encouraged, whatever doesn't is ignored. If the father is a carpenter, he will spot that talent in his child, while an academician will encourage apparently studious leanings—even if the actual abilities of the children are just the opposite.

Consequently, from a young age, two different personalities are formed: one is what we really are, and the other what we believe we must be. Naturally, the self-created persona has many strengths and hardly any weaknesses. This is in contrast to the other personality, shaped by others, that usually tends to be inclined in the opposite direction. People are seldom keen to have a strong opponent. They cut you down to size with phrases like, 'Stay within your limits,' or 'Stick to what you know.'

Self-appraisal can be a handicap

People begin from a young age to limit themselves.

What this means is that everyone decides for themselves

what they can achieve in life and where their limits are. And, in fact, then they never go further. This limit isn't due to lack of ability, it's the result of a mind block. Other people have not had your upbringing and therefore have a very different view of you.

What does recognising ability have to do with upbringing? I myself grew up with five words that I simply couldn't shake off for a long time: 'Don't blow your own trumpet.' Today I know that nobody has any interest in other people becoming aware of their own abilities.

Let us imagine that your secretary, or whoever takes your calls when you can't attend to them, tells you that the owner of one of the biggest companies in the world personally called to speak to you and is expecting a call back.

What thoughts cross your mind? And what do you do? Please write both these things in your notebook.

I reckon that a large number of people would not call back. 'Why would someone like that call me of all people? They don't even know me. More importantly, there are thousands of people out there who can do this much better than I can. I'll just make a fool of myself!'

What would the answer be according to the Shaolin principle? Just call back and see what the person has to say. Don't call with the desire to get a million-dollar contract, but also without any stress. Why should that person not have called you?

Write down the answer to this too. Do I hear a, 'Because I...?' Because you what? You don't even know yet what the caller wanted, do you? Perhaps you have abilities that you yourself were not aware of.

If people knew their own abilities, they would be independent of praise or criticism by opponents! 'You are good when I tell you that you are good. You have no way of judging that on your own. What do you even know about yourself?'

It's easy to illustrate how deep-rooted this principle is in most of us. I would even venture to say that you would find it easier to deal with a negative comment than with praise. Let's assume you show me a painting that you created as part of a course I am teaching. You consider me an expert, so my opinion is very important to you. If I were to briefly glance at the painting and immediately find something to criticise, you would probably accept it without question. Even if you really liked the painting, you would immediately work on eliminating the supposed mistakes. It was clear to you anyway that you were nowhere close to my talent, and at least I was honest with you.

But what if, after an equally brief appraisal, I was to praise your picture? If I were to tell you that it's beautiful, that I never expected you would be able to produce such work and that I would never have hit upon the idea myself?

You would immediately start wondering about the intention behind my praise. Ah, since you paid for my course, I would hardly be likely to criticise you as a client, would I?

No false modesty

It never fails to surprise me that when you ask anyone about their weaknesses, they can reel off an entire list. But a question about what they can do really well is usually met with embarrassed silence.

In the previous chapter, I tried showing you several times how opponents try to place themselves in a position superior to you without your noticing. This is possible because most people tend to measure their worth relative to others rather than in absolute terms. Either I can do something or I can't do it. That doesn't change, even if someone else apparently does it better. I should be aware of my own abilities.

EXERCISES

WHOSE JUDGEMENT COUNTS?

Please imagine that you are appearing for a practical examination. You are very good in your subject and have also prepared well. There is nothing that could take you by surprise.

Now I enter the picture as the examiner. I am introduced to you as a great master. Of course, I make a big show of this to hide the fact that I don't have the faintest clue about your subject.

You begin working. I stand next to you, look pointedly and make it very obvious that I am observing you. At one point when you perform an action that you are very sure and confident about, I start frowning and looking questioningly, followed by a slight shaking of my head and a knowing smile. Then I indicate with my hand, 'It's fine, carry on, don't let me disturb you!'

Even though you have performed that action identically a thousand times, this irritates you. 'He's looking like that, and he's an expert. Have I done something wrong?'

- Now the question: you are good and you know it. Why does my behaviour still make you uncertain? Please write this in your notebook.

Let's get back to the examination. This time I am introduced as someone who wants to learn your profession and would therefore like to watch the exam. I behave in exactly the same way as before.

Please note why you now have a different reaction. I am deliberately trying to be provocative because it really is not logical.

If you know something, you know it. It doesn't matter if your mother is standing next to you or an examiner or the president of the United States. Of course, in the latter two cases it's quite possible that there might be a degree of nervousness. But why should you suddenly start doubting whether you are doing something correctly? I will tell you why. It's because you never consciously made yourself aware that it is correct. You have not been criticised, so it cannot be wrong. But does that make it right? If no one has told you till now that you are bad, does that mean you are good?

- Who can tell you whether you are good? Please write the names of three persons, whom you would entrust with this difficult task.
- Alongside, please also write what advantage each of these persons would derive if they were not completely honest with you.

You can run away from everything in the world—from your enemies and your friends, from favourite and hated places, from your work and your hobbies. There is only person you cannot escape from: yourself. Wherever you may hide, whatever tricks you may think up, you are the person with whom you will always have to live.

Lao Tzu said, 'Knowing others is wisdom; knowing yourself is enlightenment.'

So it makes sense to get to know each other better, isn't it? To know what each can and can't expect from the other.

Self-deception doesn't pay

If we leave the moral aspect aside, we can lie to every person on earth but not to ourselves. You must always be honest with yourself, always know what is possible and what won't work.

You must never pretend anything to yourself, and also not believe the stories we tell others about ourselves.

In *The Art of War*, Sun Tzu writes, 'If you know the enemy and know yourself, you need not fear the result of a hundred battles. If you know yourself but not the enemy, for every victory gained you will also suffer a defeat. If you know neither the enemy nor yourself, you will succumb in every battle.'

EXERCISES

WHO ARE YOU REALLY?

- Please take your notebook out again. Put aside all value judgements and without overthinking find ten characteristics that best describe you.

- Under this now write ten terms your best friend would use to describe you.
- Below these, note how people who look up to you might view you.
- Now compare the three lists. Where do they diverge? Why?
- Go back to the list with your own assessment. Review each attribute and critically determine whether it actually applies. If you realise that some express only what you would like to be rather than what you are, find a replacement. What you are left with are ten characteristics that describe your personality.
- How far off the mark are other people in their assessment of you?
- Next to each of these characteristics note down how they can be of advantage and disadvantage to you. Where can you use them as a weapon and where could an opponent use them against you? Write three answers for each.

What I want to show you with this exercise is that nothing is good or bad with reference to oneself. Where there is much light, the shadow is deep. But there is also much light, that's the whole point.

The Shaolin principle teaches us that nobody can judge us or know us, only we ourselves can. Only what we consider high is really high; what we consider strong is really strong; what we consider good is actually good. We are who we make ourselves to be. We stand where we put ourselves.

How to deal with criticism

A weapon is effective only if it is correctly used. Being the world's richest person has its advantages: one has no worries about money, can afford what one desires and owns whatever money can buy. But if one is kidnapped for a ransom, wouldn't one rather be the poorest person on earth?

Regardless of how good you are at something, there will always be someone who finds a fault to pick. Learning to deal with criticism is an important ability you must possess to survive in society. It is difficult to give a general answer about the purpose of criticism. But there is no doubt that it can be used as a weapon. What is decisive is how the target of the criticism deals with it. You may reject criticism, consider it insulting, justify yourself or see it as harmful.

'I am good, so I am not interested in others' objections to what I do. I don't even listen to such comments.'

This way you miss the chance to become even better. If you really knew you were good, you would consider a critic's comments as a disguised indication of how to improve. You would convert the attacker's energy into your own. Don't forget: you do not need to please others, but you have to live with yourself. If you aren't aware of how extensive your capabilities really are, you will happily be influenced by others who tell you the opposite.

The words of an opponent obtain their emotional power from the fact that your opponent does not see you the way you would like them to.

I recall a great boxer who wanted to return to the ring after a long break to avenge a fight he lost years ago. After winning his revenge bout he recounted that everyone had advised him against it: his friends, relatives, trainer. 'It was just something I wanted to do. But nobody believed in me. I thought, when I am alone in the ring, where will they all be then? That's when I knew that I would do it, and that I would succeed.' The Shaolin principle teaches us to recognise that, ultimately, we are answerable only to ourselves. What others think of us doesn't count. All that is relevant is what we are confident of being able to do. No one besides us can take responsibility for our actions. And ultimately no one else takes responsibility for our life. Each one of us has an unlimited stock of wishes. All that is necessary is for us to create the conditions to fulfil them. 'Happiness,' it is said in China, 'is not what we want but what we are.' Or in the words of Siddhartha: 'Our life is shaped by our mind; we become what we think.'

EXERCISES

A LITTLE INTROSPECTION

The questions below should help you to become aware of yourself and what is special about you as a person.

Complete the following sentences: I can..., I think..., I believe..., I fear..., I hope...

....

What is the maximum you can achieve in life?

....

If I wanted to hire you for a managerial position in my company, which position would you apply for?

....

Why?

....

What makes you special as a person?

....

What is your biggest strength?

....

Will you become famous some time?

....

Where do you see yourself in five years?

....

You never win alone. The day you start believing something else, you start losing.

Mika Häkkinen

13. The Principle of Community

The best executive is the one who has sense enough to pick good men to do what he wants done, and self-restraint to keep from meddling with them while they do it.

Theodore Roosevelt

Learn that leadership does not mean power over others but the opportunity to achieve a common goal.

In the year 621, the abbot of the Shaolin monastery received an urgent call for help. Li Shimin, who would go on to become the first emperor of the Tang dynasty, had been captured by an enemy general and his army destroyed. The later emperor saw in the famous monks, whose martial skills he had often heard of, the only hope of being rescued. The monks themselves were already angered because the enemy had also captured some of their lands, and so the abbot decided to act. But he sent just thirteen handpicked monks against the enemy's mighty army. Their only weapons were sticks and the strength of the two monks, who were to lead. The skill of both these monks emanated from their deep insight and self-knowledge and was reflected in three major ways: belief in themselves, belief in their mission and belief that all together they could achieve their goal.

Self-leadership is crucial

There is an old saying that the first step to leadership is the ability to lead oneself.

If you want to lead others, you must first lead yourself.
If you want to know others, you must first know yourself.

It might appear that leadership is all about other people, but never forget that you are an important—probably *the* most important—part of this game. After all, it is much more worthwhile to deter a single leader and along with them thousands of their followers rather than a single soldier.

You can thus be the strongest link in your team or, by the same token, the weakest. You can become the target of many attacks and constantly be challenged to fight. Or you could learn to fight so well that you no longer need to and can utilise your energy for more important things.

> Have you ever wondered why some people literally invite being attacked, while there are others you would never dream of picking a fight with? Please write three reasons in your notebook.

In fact, this has nothing to do with actual opportunities or with position or strength. It is the same as if I were to ask if you generally keep a greater distance from persons simply because they are wearing a suit or they have an important title on their visiting card? I doubt it.

Authority depends on inner attitude

Authority has nothing to do with appearance, age, clothing, titles or position. Unassailability is something that one exudes through one's personality. And vice-versa, many people open themselves to attack because of their thoughts and fears. You might recall that when you were at school there were all kinds of teachers. Each one essentially had the same means at their disposal to discipline students: punish, summon the parents, make entries in the class register or send badly behaved students to the dreaded principal. But although the same potential weapons are available to all, only those who are unassailable are always victorious and consequently do not even need to use these weapons.

It has nothing to do with physical strength or a particular position at the school. A rebellious student has the same scant respect for a burly senior teacher as for a soft-spoken female teacher. When a teacher enters a classroom, the students react to their charisma. They size them up either as potentially weak or as a superior—and therefore impossible—opponent.

This assessment happens subconsciously, so it has nothing to do with any visible traits. A small, delicate woman can exude more authority than a muscled giant. I will forever remember my Latin teacher, who for me became the epitome of this kind of authority. She was an elderly, old-fashioned, elegant lady with an unremarkable appearance but with tremendous presence. She was the kind of person in whose presence you wouldn't just not do certain things, you wouldn't even dream of doing them. I cannot recall a single instance when she resorted to any of the disciplinary measures mentioned above or shouted or made any threats. But I also cannot remember a single occasion when I did not do my homework or behaved badly in her class. Even other students who would stand on the tables singing and shouting in other classes would undergo a complete transformation the minute she appeared. They would sit at their places with lowered heads as meek as lambs.

Nobody begins a fight with someone they consider stronger. This principle is clearly illustrated in the relationship between humans and animals. Even animals that are physically superior to humans, like cows or elephants, submit as soon as humans signal to them that a fight would be futile. On the other hand, you often hear that animals can literally smell fear in their human opponents, which actually encourages them to attack. Do you belong to the first or second category of people? Why? What do you think makes someone unassailable? Please write this down in your notebook.

Empty vessels make the most noise

Many people mistakenly believe that authority can be established by making threats. Unfortunately, quite often this seems to be true. People do what is demanded of them, at least superficially, if the consequences of non-compliance are convincingly made clear to them. However, when the threat wanes, the situation very quickly changes. A good example again is school. Be honest: how much of the knowledge that you acquired under the greatest pressure has stayed with you? What have you learnt for life, especially in those subjects that you disliked?

On the other hand, power games using threats also always involve playing with fire. If your opponent sees through the game and does not play ball, or if a person who is intrinsic to the threat does not react along expected lines, then you can no longer carry out the threat. You would lose more than just face. Let's assume you are a teacher. You carry out your ultimate threat and send a student who refuses to listen to you to the feared principal. Contrary to your expectation, the principal does not find the case so bad and does warn the child, but in a friendly way. The child returns and tells the entire class that the principal was much nicer than everyone believed and they would gladly be sent there again. Do you understand why you would now have a problem?

In this context, I recall a situation that occurred during my compulsory military service. The commanding officer of our group was one of those people who believe they can establish authority with threats. One evening, there was yet another argument between that CO and one of the recruits. This ended in the young man being ordered to pack all his belongings in his rucksack and turn up before the barracks in an impossibly short time. The officer threatened that if he did not, he would have the recruit arrested. The threat worked initially as the young man desperately tried to comply with the order, which however he was unable to despite all of us pitching in. Things took their inevitable turn. The CO, accompanied by two armed guards, came into our room and planted himself before the recruit. We all waited with bated breath, wondering how this power game would play out.

'Recruit X,' the commanding officer barked, 'according to rule so and so you are hereby arrested and…' 'Don't waste your breath,' the recruit interrupted him, 'I know your stupid statements.' He went off with the guards without any further protest, joking as he left. After a night in the cell, X was found unfit for and exempted from military service. The commanding officer's completely over-the-top behaviour made him lose a lot of his authority.

If you are truly a leader, your colleagues will stand by you even in situations where they could stab you in the back without suffering any consequences.

In reality, threats are not just useless, they are usually also dangerous. As noted above, if you attempt to change a colleague's behaviour by threatening them with dire consequences, you will almost certainly be successful to start with. As long as your colleague accepts that you are more powerful in a given situation, they will obey your instructions, perhaps even without protest. But the issue with the 'authority through pressure' method is that the battle is only seemingly won. A time will come when the tables turn and the power equation reverses.

Win over with arguments

I find it interesting in this context that many people misunderstand democracy to be an alien concept for members of one of the world's largest religious communities. I say misunderstand because rejection of democracy does not necessarily mean acceptance of dictatorship. Quite to the contrary. Long before there was any semblance of Islam as a religion in what is today the Arab world, people there lived in tribes that were hostile to one another. War and fighting were so commonplace that a tribe's survival depended on its ability to motivate individual members to hold together at all costs. Everyone needed to know what had to be done and why, and each one had to have an interest in the survival of the tribe. The elders were convinced that anyone who had to bow to the pressure of the democratic majority would use the first opportunity to harm it. Consequently, for all important decisions, discussions and arguments were employed rather than threats. This ensured that everyone could act according to their own convictions and in the interests of the community.

Vanity weakens opponents

A totally different line of attack is vanity. Someone who feels flattered tends to evaluate facts emotionally because they are pleased, thereby opening themselves to manipulation. An insurance agent who enters your house and enthusiastically exclaims, 'What a lovely place you have!' can count on a more congenial response from you than a colleague who refrains from this flattery and comes straight to business.

People want to be told that you see them as what they believe they are or what they aspire to be.

For instance, nobody would take an extremely expensive watch that they absolutely must possess to a desolate island where no one will see it. For some people, getting recognition is so important that they often lose sight of the goal.

Take the example of Company X. One striking feature about the company is that every employee has a more or less important title. I don't mean academic titles or designations like art director or managing director, but titles such as assistant head of department or senior office supervisor. These are titles that the concerned employees have received as an incentive. Now, employee Y on the orders of his boss asks for two quotations for a particular service. Company A, which has the obviously better offer but is not aware of the special customs in our company replies, 'Dear Mr Y, with reference to your enquiry, we would like to offer…'. On the other hand, the offer from Company B is clearly inferior, but it is addressed to the 'Head of the Department' and thanks Mr Y for his very kind enquiry. Which quotation will Y present to his boss? And why does it matter to Y if he is not addressed by his title?

Write three kinds of compliments in your notebook with which you can be manipulated.

The technique of 'overpraising'

An additional attack technique that makes use of vanity is what I call 'overpraising'. This is dangerous for two reasons: one, because often it is imperceptible; and second because victims cannot defend themselves against it. Let us assume that A works for your company in a department in which I would like to work. I know about A, but I apply to you nonetheless. My objective is to use you to displace A. During the interview you let me know that you already have someone working in that area. However, to lay a trap for me you suddenly say that a project is likely to come up shortly that might be too difficult for A to handle and ask if I would be willing to take it on. Knowing A, I could tell you that you are actually right. But your intention isn't to entrust the work to me because you believe that A can do it. You merely want to test my reaction. This is where vanity comes into play. If I were to criticise A, you would perceive it as criticism of yourself and your decision to hire A. So even though I know that A is not capable of handling the project, I cannot convey this to you. Anything negative I say would be held against me because obviously someone who wants the job will try to badmouth their competitors… Your judgement consequently is not based on facts but on vanity. You selected the employee, so of course you know what they are capable of! How do I still manage to get a foot in? I need to let you learn the hard way by appealing to this vanity. Instead of showing interest, I would reject the idea, horrified, 'If A is working in this position, then they would surely know how to handle this. A is one of the best people for this job that I can think of! Of course, you hired him so you know that best. You definitely don't need me for this job!' I would project A to be much better than A actually is. You are satisfied because you have heard what you wanted to hear. Expectedly, A will not be able to deliver because the project is beyond their capabilities. This causes you actual harm. Your vanity made it impossible for me to warn you. Simultaneously, it served me as a weapon against A. Through my praise, your impression of A became even better, so naturally your disappointment at A's failure was all the greater. You subsequently stop working with A. Since you still remember me, I now receive an assignment from you—this time on my terms.

There are, in fact, many ways to win without a fight by using the 'overpraising' technique. Follow me briefly to a job interview. Since this is an extremely important position, a senior member of the board of directors is present apart from the head of the department, who will ask technical questions. If I now want to show up the technical expert in front of the boss, I will simply think of a question to which the expert will almost certainly not have an answer. 'I know,' I begin innocently, 'that this is a dumb question, but since we have the experts here… you surely know how…' Of course they don't. And the boss will form their own opinion.

The technique of provocation

Another vulnerability that is similar to vanity and equally dangerous is allowing oneself to get provoked. In an earlier chapter I introduced you to a closely related technique: the mock attack. I'm sure you are familiar with attacks along the lines of, 'I always knew you couldn't do it…' These are especially dangerous because the attacker's real intentions become apparent much later.

Let's say I ask you to work on ideas for a new business division. You come up with such good ideas that you decide it would be much more profitable for you to sell these elsewhere. When I question you about your progress you reply that you couldn't come up with any ideas. My reaction could now be combative: I could confront you directly and let you know that I am aware of your true intentions. You would immediately be warned since you would be able to read my intent. So let's try another way. 'You know, H, I didn't actually expect you to succeed. Perhaps it was also too difficult a task for you. Worth a try, but this outcome was to be expected.' 'What do you mean too difficult? Do you think that just because I don't have a fancy position, I'm not capable? It's not as if I haven't come up with any ideas! I just wanted a little more time to polish them, but since you insist, here's the document.' There you are: you've won without a fight.

Used correctly, provocation is a very powerful technique. In the situation above, you were probably expecting to be pulled up and asked to submit your work or face the consequences. You were prepared for that and were ready with a counter strategy. I would never have managed to get the document from you. But since I provoked your vanity, you were diverted from the actual issue. You became careless and consequently turned into an easy opponent. Conversely, the technique of provocation can also be used to motivate. Asking—'You know, that would be great, but do you really believe you can still manage that?'—can often work wonders.

Winning without fighting requires you to focus your energy on reaching the goal rather than on looking good in the process.

The *Tao Te Ching* says, 'If you overcome others, you are powerful; if you overcome yourself, you have strength.' Leadership is not about power but it is very much about strength. Even a hungry tiger will not hunt the strongest or most dangerous-looking zebra but will look for one that is young, weak or already injured. The tiger's objective is to satiate his hunger, not to be regarded as a brave hunter. For animals this behaviour is natural. But, as discussed above, many people don't follow this path because their weakness is vanity.

Lao Tzu said, 'A wise man does only what needs to be done to achieve victory. He does not use violence to dominate the enemy.'

This is a blind spot for many victors. The desire to destroy the opponent, to punish them for the attack takes over and becomes an obsession. It distorts their perception of what is of essence.

Not displaying power means to show strength

'A good fighter does not seek revenge,' is a common saying at the Shaolin monastery. A good leader or a good manager must also know where to draw the line. For a good leader, victory consists in getting things done, never in gaining power over others.

Let's go back to the example above. My goal was to obtain the document with your ideas, which you did not want to give me. As soon as I get the document I have won and it's time to stop. After all, you will in all likelihood continue to have good ideas in the future. If I were to withdraw at this stage by heaping praise on you, neither of us would lose face. On the contrary, you will probably feel proud about having shown me how I underestimated my colleagues.

You will not be unhappy or angered at your loss, which in any case isn't one, strictly speaking. A bad response in this situation would have been if I reacted purely emotionally on realising that an employee was trying to suppress information. Shouting and threats would have been counter-productive. All I would achieve would be to turn you into an enemy because you would feel outsmarted. What would I gain? Consequently, any action I take prompted by feelings of anger and disappointment would be wrong.

You could be reading this and thinking, 'Now isn't it a bit much if I have to use tricks to get something that I'm already paying for!' You may not like to hear this, but this is the way things sometimes are.

As the saying goes in Shaolin, winning without a fight can be achieved through the path of least resistance. Always remember that you must be guided only by what is necessary, never by emotions and personal vanities. And don't forget to stop at the point where you achieve your goal.

Wu Wei: Doing by non-doing

Often, the path of least resistance is one that is achieved by a technique known as *wu wei* in Shaolin. In English this means something like 'doing by non-doing'. If the goal is to win a battle and this can be achieved without fighting, why then should one fight? Not showing a reaction is also a reaction: it allows the opponent's force to be redirected.

I would like to give you an example. You happen to witness an accident and someone approaches you for your contact details so that you can testify if the case goes to court. You don't want to go to court or have anything further to do with the matter and say so directly to this person. You tell them that you never appear as a witness on principle and mention previous bad experiences. The person insists that you must. An argument ensues and finally the police comes and takes down your details. You must now convince the court of your principles. If you finally manage not to be made to testify, it would have cost you much time and energy to make your views known to a large number of people. But you would not have achieved your actual goal, which was not to be involved in the matter. This you could have achieved much more simply. All you needed to reply was, 'Yes, of course I would be very happy to help, but I happened to look at my phone at just that moment and didn't see what happened…' The matter would have been closed then and there.

Leadership means responsibility

Many people believe that leadership is synonymous with forcing people to do something or restricting their freedom against their will. Actually, it is just the opposite. Most people want to be led. Entire industries are based on this fact: tour operators, associations, lawmakers, travel guides, political parties, armies, companies, etc. If freedom were as important as it is often portrayed to be, probably nobody would be employed and everyone would be their own boss. But that's not the case. Why? For one, because people like to follow the easy path. Whether we like it or not, we have become a 'society of choice'. A few people determine the options from which the mass of people selects. This is true at a macro and micro level, where it is especially obvious. Even on our computers we no longer enter commands ourselves; we choose from a menu of options and don't even think about whether there could be any more possibilities. The flip side is that hardly anyone wants to take any responsibility.

George Bernard Shaw once said, 'Liberty means responsibility. That is why most men dread it.'

Wanting to lead people thus has nothing to do with power or violence. It is a very natural principle, just as fighting is.

Fighting is part of survival

It might not be politically correct to say so today, but fighting is natural and this must be accepted. Even if you yourself do not attack because you want to avoid fighting, you will often be the target of attacks. To win without fighting, it is first essential to accept that fighting exists. It is a part of life. After all, fighting—or rather the associated victory—is nature's incentive to keep improving. Everything that has had to prove its worth did so in a combat. Denying the existence of fighting is like crossing the highway with your eyes closed and hoping that nothing will happen. Fighting is all pervasive: the fight for survival, the struggle for jobs, the battle of the sexes, competition…

A quote attributed to Bertold Brecht says:

'What if they gave a war and no one came? Then the war will come to you.'

Here is an example: one day a person receives a notice from the police for speeding. The notice states that objections can be filed within fourteen days, otherwise the notice becomes legally binding. This person, who neither has a car nor a driving licence and so can't have been involved, thinks, 'It wasn't me so they can't do anything,' and consequently doesn't file an objection. The truth that needs to be recognised here is that 'not having done something' and 'not being punished' are two completely different things in some legal systems. Naturally, the law will take its course, the deadline for appeal will pass and this person will be convicted and have to pay a fine for an offence that they did not commit. But they committed something else—they ignored a fight. They themselves did not attack, but they were attacked.

Had they been prepared to see the truth and responded to the attack immediately, the matter would probably have been resolved. Essentially, it was the attitude of not-wanting-to-see what the issue was that turned it into a problem.

Communication is key

One of the most important tasks by far that leaders have is to set clear goals and to communicate these effectively. In Shaolin, it is known that leaders must not be superficial and convoluted in their thinking. Clearsighted, simple thinking and communication are essential.

Fighters who haven't thought about where precisely they intend to target their adversary will hit air or crash to the ground before they can even land their first blow. Soldiers who receive only half the information will never be able to deploy their full strength.

When you need to explain the goals and way to achieve them to your colleagues, remember the most important rule at all times: never assume anything. To put it bluntly: if one of your colleagues does not do something or doesn't know something because you did not explain it to them assuming it was clear, the fault is yours. Apart from making that person feel unsure, you will lose time and energy in correcting the mistake. On the other hand, if your communication is clear and uncomplicated, your colleagues will feel comfortable with you.

A leader's competence also includes giving the impression that they know the goal and the path to achieve it, even when the going gets tough. Don't forget: people want to be led. That is why they have put themselves in your charge.

We all want to be led, and you yourself are no exception. Let's imagine you visit a portrait photographer. You obviously expect that they will instruct you on how you should sit or stand, how to place your hands and which way you should look. You readily trust that the photographs will show you in the best light and you will be happy with the end result. But if the photographer makes you feel that they have no idea about how you should pose, if they keep trying out various things, you will not be convinced by the results, even if the pictures are the same as those of the first photographer. Incidentally, this doesn't mean that all photographers always know what is needed and how to do it. But most of them will give you the impression that they do, and this will make you feel you got good service and you will be happy to come back. Ultimately, the photographer 'led' you to a good picture. Of course, nobody can really know what needs to be done in every conceivable situation. In fact, it isn't even that important as long as they can give the impression that they do.

Leaders must give recognition

Let's go back to the photographer mentioned above. You want to get pictures taken for a company brochure. The photographer makes you pose but then they shake their head and don't take the picture. What thoughts go through your head? Would you not feel much better if the photographer took a picture of each new pose even if they weren't satisfied, and only then went on to the next shot?

It becomes easy to lead people if we remember one of the fundamental principles of nature: practically all living beings seek appreciation and will do everything to get it.

This ranges from fights for dominance in the animal kingdom to office intrigues. What matters is to be one up on others. This need can be satisfied if one is able to make it to the top or—more commonly—if one is liked by others. This desire is very strong among most of us, obvious from people needing to have status symbols for which they are admired by others. If you don't believe me, please honestly answer this question: two trousers are available for the same price. They both look the same, were made in the same factory and are absolutely identical in quality. The only difference is that one trouser has the label of a very expensive brand. It is basically a designer garment. Which of the two would you choose for yourself? Why?

Recognition is not necessarily related to material value. Even children are proud of the all-knowing adults they can call 'their own'. What wouldn't many employees give to have the CEO of the company personally praising their work? Praise from the top is like a handshake with the king. This principle has been known for a long time. In the mid-eighteenth century, the French writer Vauvenargues wrote, 'To praise moderately is always a sign of mediocrity.'

A person who is in a position to give recognition to others can also control them.

Many people want to be led because they like having role models. Someone they can look up to, through whom they can vicariously live their dreams. When you are a leader, you are exactly in this position whether you like it or not. It is a great opportunity, but also a great responsibility.

Being aware of responsibility

Never forget that the person at the very top has the power to help people rise but also to push them down. The latter probably happens more often due to carelessness than intent. Many managers are often not aware of the extent of their power. Imagine that after an already difficult day, you learn that one of your products is facing problems in country X. Frustrated and angry, you start cursing the country and calling its citizens nitwits. What do you achieve? People who are familiar with you will think you're having a bad day, but apart from that your statements will have no consequences. Imagine now, that you are the president of a superpower and use exactly these words in a similar situation. If you're lucky, your gaffe will only make it to newspaper front pages. This is how it is at every level. Let's face it: Your neighbour's son criticising the work of an employee and the head of the company doing so is certainly not the same thing.

Leadership means winning together

The two monks at the beginning of this chapter may have been very strong, but it is highly doubtful that they would have been able to achieve victory alone. Their real strength were their eleven colleagues and the ability of the leaders to deploy them correctly. During subsequent battles into which the monastery was drawn, the monks did not do the actual fighting themselves. Instead, they motivated and trained people who happened to be available. Most of them were local farmers. Perhaps the monks would have preferred experienced soldiers, but there were none available. The monks knew it didn't matter who they were fighting alongside, all that mattered was what their leaders made of them. That is a leader's job.

Another strength of the leadership council of the monastery was the decision to accept anyone as a monk who could contribute to the development of the monastic community. Neither a biodata nor references were necessary, simply an interest and a willingness to share one's knowledge. Thus, in addition to virtuous novices, the Shaolin temple also accepted people that no other monastery wanted. The monks did not attempt to reform these people; they made use of their knowledge, their skill and also their unique qualities.

'Focus on what you have.' This is one of the most important precepts in Shaolin. Do not complain about what you do not have. Make the best of what you do.

If you think you don't have the right employees, make sure that they become those. Employees are not your opponents, they are your weapons. There are no good or bad employees. Each one of them is as good as your knowledge of them and your ability to use them.

I was told the following story about this when I was in Shaolin. A monk went to the market and heard a conversation between a butcher and a customer. 'Give me your best piece of meat,' said the customer. 'Everything in my shop is the best,' replied the butcher, 'you will not find a single piece of meat in my shop that is not the best.' Hearing these words, the monk was enlightened.

Regard your work as a manager as a journey with your employees, in which you can only reach your destination together. Your job is to delegate to each employee what they will best be able to accomplish by utilising all their skill, knowledge and talent.

Robert Lembke, a German journalist and TV host, put it this way: 'You can gauge the skill of a boss by their skill in gauging the skills of their employees.' Many managers are not sufficiently flexible in this respect to be able to extract the best from each employee.

Let's take the example of P, who is assigned to you as telephone operator by the HR department. The very first call that P answers is enough to tell you that communication is not their forte. But because P has been designated for this position by HR, you insist that P must learn, even if Q is in a position that would be perfect for P and Q would prefer to do P's job.

I remember one colleague, whose true potential I didn't recognise for a long time. T was someone who could achieve brilliant results if given clear instructions but was utterly incapable of working without them. It was useless to tell T, 'Think about who would be the best person to contact for this.' Initially, this would lead to no result and much frustration. But if I said to T, 'Contact the president of the United States and make sure that I get an appointment with him tomorrow,' I could be certain that the president would not just be informed but would also be waiting to receive me.

With such employees it is especially important to take the time to listen to their successes and never to forget to praise them. Without an opportunity for feedback, such employees often feel their task is incomplete.

Employees are neither 'good' nor 'bad'

It is fundamentally true that fellow human beings, superiors and colleagues are neither good nor bad. Quite apart from the fact that this kind of categorisation depends entirely on a subjective point of view, no person only wishes you good or only cheats you. The question rather is whether you are ready to accept each person you meet in life as they really are and not as you imagine them to be. If you aren't prepared to do this, a person who is filed away in your system of evaluation as 'good' will continue to be good regardless of what they do. Even if this person attempted to deceive you, you would find a hundred reasons why this couldn't be, you would hold others responsible and do everything so you didn't have to see the truth. When you are finally forced to do so, this person will move into the category of 'disappointments' forever, and they can never again be in your good books.

Vice versa, you will not be prepared to accept anything from a colleague you have categorised as 'incompetent', because nothing they do can be good in your eyes. It's the same with your colleagues. Many managers consider an employee who couldn't do a certain job properly to be generally incompetent. In his book *Enchiridion*, the Greek philosopher Epictetus writes:

'If a man washes quickly, do not say that he washes badly, but that he washes quickly. If a man drinks much wine, do not say that he drinks badly, but that he drinks much. For till you have decided what judgement prompts him, how do you know that he acts badly? If you do as I say, you will assent to your apprehensive impressions and to none other.'

So, in the case of the apparently incompetent employee, Epictetus would probably have said, 'Do not say that he is incapable, but that he is not suited for this task.' After all, nobody is suited for everything but at the same time nobody is suited for nothing.

It is therefore important to observe each person anew, objectively and without emotion. Even persons you simply cannot understand, who have made a hash of everything that could conceivably have been made a hash of, might just be *the* person for the job at hand.

Never lose sight of the truth

The Chinese philosopher Chuang Tzu said, 'For travelling by water there is nothing like a boat. This is because a boat moves readily in water; but were you to try to push it on land you would never succeed in making it go: great trouble and no result, except certain injury to oneself.'

Seeing the truth means to take a step back and see things and people exactly as they are at that moment. This truth is independent of how you feel about a person, whether you like them or not. Those who do not want to see the truth make themselves vulnerable and open to attack.

Sometimes it is easier and more convenient to continue to stick to one's beliefs, but this is what you must avoid doing. The same applies to your employees. If someone you like is late for work, he must have had to attend to an important call or something else that excuses his coming in late. But if that person is someone you have made into a personal enemy, you will consider each explanation to be an excuse and your reaction will be accusatory. Although the employee arrived late in both cases, your emotions distort your perception of the truth and you might end up not taking necessary steps.

At the same time, it is extremely important for managers to see the truth even where they themselves are concerned. A product that is not selling because it is a bad product remains a bad product and this should be accepted. It doesn't matter if you or the CEO piloted the product. Explanations like, 'wrong timing' or 'poor marketing' are a waste of energy in such cases. This energy would be better utilised in improving the product. Even misbehaviour by a manager is misbehaviour, which you should admit to, at least to yourself. Otherwise it may become a habit.

Always utilise the talents of the best

A general who intends to lead his army to a victory without fighting will take the strongest and best soldiers he can get. What seems so obvious in theory doesn't always happen in practice. Many bosses don't fight alongside their colleagues but against them, and thus ultimately against themselves. Many managers tend to think, 'This colleague would be good for the job, but they are much better in this field than I am. If I take them then I might lose my position. Let me take someone not as capable, that's less risky.' Everyone is seen as a potential competitor who is vying to become the boss.

Even at the top management level, there is often the fear that employees might use knowledge they obtain to start their own company and become competition. Quite apart from the fact that this kind of fear is an energy sapper, let me assure you that it's something you can't prevent anyway. So, utilise the capabilities of the best people to achieve your goals and allow them to keep improving in the interests of your company.

Another negative fall-out of this restrictive approach is that very little knowledge is shared. Performance rapidly drops in departments that are led by managers with this attitude. Restricting access to knowledge can be a very useful measure vis-à-vis competitors, but in your own company it can have very negative consequences. Even if each of your employees could theoretically mutate into a competitor, they aren't one at this very moment.

Strong leadership means reaching your goal together with the people you are leading. Armed with this knowledge, a group of thirteen monks were able to defeat an entire army. They achieved even more: by applying this knowledge, the group made themselves and the Shaolin temple immortal.

EXERCISES

IDENTIFY YOUR LEADERSHIP STRENGTHS

1. Please imagine that you are a professional graphic designer. One day, you receive an opportunity to design the logo and complete brand identity of a multinational company. Before the job can be completed, the company's management changes and the new board of directors wants to engage another graphic designer. The company makes the following offer to you: either you will receive just half the agreed amount and the company will use your design globally, or you receive double the payment and your work will be filed away and never used. Which

option would you choose if you were

(a) a freelance graphic designer;
(b) boss of an agency with 50 employees, and why?

2. You are a manager and have employees from all departments. How quickly could you tell me which of these

   (a) is an expert with computers;
   (b) can write excellent advertising copy;
   (c) could professionally videograph the company's celebration party?

3. Which of your colleagues could negotiate with a client with whom you yourself have not been able to establish a rapport?
4. During an argument, a colleague says you are incompetent to lead the department. How would you react if this was

   (a) a superior;
   (b) a person reporting to you?

   - If you react differently in both cases, why?
   - Would you assess this colleague's performance differently from now on?

5. At which position could an employee whom you consider the least useful help your team to achieve victory?

6. Do any of your employees not work in areas where they have maximum strengths?

Why?

7. You are a private individual who has purchased defective goods from a company. Your claim against the company is justified and the company does not deny it, but refuses to do anything. You are considering going to court but hear from a friend that the company has very good lawyers. Does this influence your decision to file a case? (Note: if you decide not to file for this reason, the company will have won without a fight.)
8. Think of five situations in your work routine in which you can only win by doing nothing!
9. Think of five important issues where you do not like to see the truth!
10. Please make two columns in your notebook. In the left column, write ten skills, one below the other, which your 'dream team' should possess (e.g. a good artist, a good speaker, a good strategist...). Please focus only on what you would wish for. Now, in the right column write down which of your colleagues has precisely these skills.
11. In which situation have you been forced to make concessions to someone because they had provoked you to do something you didn't intend to?

Epilogue

Our common journey comes to an end at this point. It was lovely to get to know you and to share a part of your life. You have now learnt a lot about people and a lot about yourself. You would also have learnt to stand, to fight and you will learn to win.

Always remember, the purpose is not the destination but the journey itself. To that end, live your life serenely and be mindful of the moment. Learn from your opponents and be aware at all times that power is not something that you will get but that you must seize. Experience how you are more self-assured when you know your worth. If you want to renew yourself, then keep at it every day!

Best wishes,
Bernhard Moestl

Shaolin Draws on Many Sources

Buddha

It is not known for certain when Siddhartha Gautama, who later called himself Buddha, really lived. Current research assumes that Gautama was born in 450 BCE in Lumbini, which is in present-day Nepal.

In his father's palace, Gautama leads a sheltered childhood, shielded from all worldly suffering to the extent that the streets are cleared of the old, sick and dying before the young Gautama ventures out. And yet, his encounter with an old man, an ill man, a decaying corpse and finally a monk change his life forever. At the age of twenty-nine, he becomes aware that wealth and luxury do not guarantee happiness. He realises that suffering, i.e., old age, sickness, death and pain, are inextricably bound with life. He decides to leave and discover the true nature of human happiness. He leaves his wife, his only son and his home and becomes an ascetic.

He wanders through the Ganges valley for six years. For six years he subjects himself to the severest practices of famous religious teachers. He almost dies in the process, but this does not bring him nearer to the object of his search. Finally, he gives up other religions and seeks his own path, which he ultimately finds in meditation.

When he is thirty-five years old, Siddhartha Gautama finally achieves absolute enlightenment sitting under a *bodhi* tree on the banks of the Niranjana River. He then names himself Buddha, which means 'the awakened'. Five of his faithful followers are witness to his first sermon, in which he reveals to them the Four Noble Truths.

The Four Noble Truths

The First Noble Truth, the monks learn, is the truth of suffering. The *chakra* of life entails suffering. The cause of suffering, as the Second Noble Truth explains, is desire, aversion and ignorance.

The Third Noble Truth states that if the causes cease, suffering will cease.

The path to ending desire and thereby suffering is charted out in the Fourth Noble Truth, also known as the Noble Eightfold Path. The end of suffering can be attained through

Right Understanding, Right Thought, Right Speech, Right Action, Right Livelihood, Right Effort, Right Mindfulness and Right Concentration.

From that day on, the Buddha preached for forty-five years to men and women of all social classes, to kings and farmers, priests and outcasts, money lenders and beggars, saints and robbers. The path that he taught was open to all men and women if they were prepared to understand and follow it.

It is said that at the age of eighty years, Gautama died of dysentery after consuming food that had gone bad. His wisdom and his truths about life and suffering were initially passed on orally by his followers and recorded in writing only 300 years after his death. Today, the religion Buddhism has about 400 million adherents in all parts of the world.

Shaolin Monastery

The Shaolin monastery—which translates into something like, 'temple in the young forest'—lies in the heart of China in the Henan province, halfway between Beijing and Hong Kong. The monastery's history goes back to 495 CE, when the emperor had it built for the Indian monk Batuo (Buddhabhadra).

Martial arts as a form of meditation

In 527, another Indian monk, Bodhidharma reached Shaolin and achieved enlightenment after nine years of sitting continuously in a cave. He taught the monks meditation.

Zen Buddhism, the path to sudden awakening, was born. When Bodhidharma, who had rudimentary training in martial arts, saw that the monks had grown fat and clumsy sitting in meditation, sometimes for days on end, he developed 'meditation through movement'. The tolerant monastery become a meeting point for martial arts experts from the entire empire. In the course of time, the art of fighting without weapons, the Shaolin kempo, achieved unparalleled perfection.

Army of monks

In 728, at the request of the Tang ruler, the monastery sent thirteen monks to support the dynasty, which was under threat from rebels. The rebellion was suppressed by the warrior monks and the monastery was granted the privilege of maintaining its own army. The monastery and its form of martial arts reached their zenith from 1368 to 1644. The ruling Ming dynasty patronised the monks and the monastery's army numbered 2500. Branch monasteries were established in China, Korea, Japan and other neighbouring countries.

The monastery was destroyed, plundered and rebuilt several times during its existence. During the great fire of 1928, a large part of the temple and even the legendary library burnt down.

Decline and revival

After the founding of the People's Republic of China by Mao Zedong in 1949, the monks were initially left alone, but during the Cultural Revolution after 1966, the temple was destroyed and the monks were persecuted and driven away. A few monks continued to stay in the ruins of the monastery for several years. It was only in 1982 that the monastery became known in the West through the film 'Shaolin Temple' and turned into a tourist destination.

The Chinese government had the temple rebuilt and in the wake of the general liberalisation of religious practices, it allowed Buddhist monks to practise their faith there once again.

Taijiquan (Tai Chi Chuan)

Taijiquan, which is also known as Chinese shadow boxing, was a form of martial arts first developed during the time of the Chinese empire.

Today, *Tai Chi*—usually in a very simplified form—is a national sport. In the mornings one can see thousands of people practising it in city parks.

Flowing movements

The essence of *Tai Chi* are the 'forms' or postures. These are clearly defined sequences of flowing movements. Each form consists of several individual movements or postures that are also called pictures. These help learners to remember the movements. The pictures have names such as, 'rhinoceros gazes at the moon', 'embrace the moon in the chest' or 'wild horse leaps over the mountain stream'.

Many forms are also named according to the number of postures, for instance the 24-form Tai Chi Chuan or the Cheng Ma Ching 37-form. The long forms have over 100 postures.

The execution of a form can take from a few minutes to an hour and a half, depending on the number of postures and the speed of execution. *Tai Chi* forms are usually executed slowly and smoothly, typically a sequence of slow and soft followed by quick, jerky movements.

Confucius

Master Kong Fu-Zi, whom the Jesuits later called Confucius, was born into an old aristocratic family in the state of Lu in the year 551 BCE. It is known that his father died when he was three and he was brought up by his mother.

Disciples compile his teachings

Although he grew up in poor circumstances, he learned the Six Arts, namely archery, charioteering, calligraphy, arithmetic, dance and music. He married at nineteen and soon thereafter became a father. He first worked as a supervisor in the public granaries and later also began to teach. In 516 BCE, Confucius was exiled. On his return to Lu he was made an administrative official and finally a minister. His strict belief in virtue and morality, which he also attempted to politically implement, made him unpopular with the ruling class and he lost his positions.

He devoted himself to writing until his death in 479 BCE. Since he never wrote down any of his own teachings, the only record is *The Analects*, a book of conversations that his students compiled.

Lao Tzu

Not much is known about Lao Tzu, whose name means 'old master'. The founder of Taoism was probably born around 600 BCE. He worked as the keeper of archives in Luoyang, the capital of the Zhou dynasty. He left the city when he foresaw the chaos and decline of the kingdom. On his travels through modern-day China, he was requested by a man named Yin Xi to share his knowledge. Thereupon, Lao Tzu wrote this down in a collection that is known today as the *Tao Te Ching*.

Legend has it that after writing the *Tao Te Ching*, Lao Tzu, who reportedly reached the age of 200 years, vanished towards the west. However, the scarcity of source material has caused historians to doubt whether Lao Tzu actually existed.

Sun Tzu

Little is known about the life of Sun Tzu, who was born around 530 BCE in the kingdom of Qi. Son of a nobleman, Sun Tzu became famous for his treatise *The Art of War*, which he wrote for King Ho-Lu of Wu.

One day, the king invited him to discuss his work and also to put him to the test. He commanded him to train the 180 women in his harem into soldiers. Sun Tzu divided the women into two companies and appointed both the favourite concubines of the king as commandants. When he gave the order for the companies to begin a drill, the girls began laughing. When even a second order elicited the same reaction, he had the two commandants executed. After that all the concubines followed his orders.

The king recognised Sun Tzu's capabilities and appointed

him general of his army. Sun Tzu died in 450 BCE, although nothing further is known about his last days.

Miyamoto Musashi

Miyamoto Musashi was born in 1548 to a rural samurai in the village of Miyamoto in Japan. When he was just thirteen years old, he is said to have killed his first opponent, a samurai well versed in fighting with the sword and spear. The young Musashi flung his opponent to the ground and subsequently smashed a stick on his head.

When he was sixteen, young Musashi set off on a journey that would take him across Old Japan. He took part in six wars and won sixty duels. By the age of twenty, Musashi was considered invincible.

The samurai then hung up his sword and began to concentrate on the inner path of swordsmanship. He learned from the samurai and the *ronin*, who came to his village, and studied many duels. Finally, he founded his own school of swordsmanship called *Niten Ichi-Ryu*. Later on, Musashi was also known as an artist and craftsman. He painted folding screens, was a master of calligraphy and created metal sculptures.

Towards the end of his life, Musashi withdrew to a cave to write the *Gorin no Sho*, or *The Book of Five Rings*. On 13 June 1645, a few weeks after he had handed the manuscript to his student Terao Magonojo, Musashi died.

Bibliography

Andy James: *The Spiritual Legacy of Shaolin Temple*. Wisdom Publications 2004.

Christopher A. Weidner: *Wabi Sabi. Nicht perfekt und trotzdem glücklich*. Droemer Knaur 2006.

Gabriele Gener: *Zen für die Achtsamkeit. Ein Schritt, ein Weg, eine Reise*. Ars Edition 2005.

Lao Tzu: *Tao Te King. Das Heilige Buch vom Tao*. (*Tao Te Ching. The Holy Book of Tao*). Schirmer 2005.

Miyamoto Musashi: *Das Buch der fünf Ringe. Die klassische Anleitung für strategisches Handeln* (*The Book of Five Rings*). Piper 2006.

Niccolò Machiavelli: *The Prince*.

Steve DeMasco: *The Shaolin Way: 10 Modern Secrets of Survival from a Shaolin Kung Fu Grandmaster*. Harper 2005.

Sun Tzu: *The Art of War*.

Volker Zotz: *Buddha. Mit Selbstzeugnissen und Bilddokumenten*. Rowohlt Tb. 2005.

Acknowledgements

Most book covers carry only the name of the actual author even though there are always many people behind a book, without whom such a project would be impossible.

My heartfelt thanks to the following: Jian Wang, who arranged my very first personal meeting with the monks of Shaolin, and Grandmaster Shi De Cheng, who was extremely patient in helping me to understand and appreciate the essence of Shaolin kung fu. Also, Heidi Mischinger, Marianne Mohatscheck, Irene Nemeth, Albert Klebel, Rainald Edel and Markus Gollner, who helped me to reflect on my ideas in countless conversations and also read my manuscript several times. I am deeply grateful to my grandmother Erika Möstl, who taught me so many of the really important things in life; and to Gerhard Conzelmann and Karl Däullary, who presented my ideas to the right people at my publishers Droemer Knaur Verlag. And finally my thanks go to Bettina Huber, Marion Ónodi and Veronika Preisler for their very kind support and the beautiful design of this book.

Index